TWO OF A KIND

RETURN TO LIGHTHOUSE POINT

KAY CORRELL

ZURA LU PUBLISHING LLC

Published by Zura Lu Publishing LLC

012520

This book is dedicated to all the people who believe in the power of wishes… and then go chase after their dreams.

Find more information on all my books at
kaycorrell.com

COMFORT CROSSING ~ THE SERIES

The Shop on Main - Book One
The Memory Box - Book Two
The Christmas Cottage - A Holiday Novella
(Book 2.5)
The Letter - Book Three
The Christmas Scarf - A Holiday Novella
(Book 3.5)
The Magnolia Cafe - Book Four
The Unexpected Wedding - Book Five

The Wedding in the Grove - (a crossover short

story between series - with Josephine and Paul from The Letter.)

LIGHTHOUSE POINT ~ THE SERIES
Wish Upon a Shell - Book One
Wedding on the Beach - Book Two
Love at the Lighthouse - Book Three
Cottage near the Point - Book Four
Return to the Island - Book Five
Bungalow by the Bay - Book Six

CHARMING INN ~ Return to Lighthouse Point
One Simple Wish - Book One
Two of a Kind - Book Two
Three Little Things - Book Three
Four Short Weeks - Book Four
Five Years or So - Book Five

SWEET RIVER ~ THE SERIES
A Dream to Believe in - Book One
A Memory to Cherish - Book Two
A Song to Remember - Book Three
A Time to Forgive - Book Four
A Summer of Secrets - Book Five
A Moment in the Moonlight - Book Six

INDIGO BAY ~ A multi-author sweet romance series

Sweet Days by the Bay - Kay's Complete Collection of stories in the Indigo Bay series

Or buy them separately:

Sweet Sunrise - Book Three
Sweet Holiday Memories - A short holiday story
Sweet Starlight - Book Nine

Sign up for my newsletter at my website *kaycorrell.com* to make sure you don't miss any new releases or sales.

CHAPTER 1

Charlotte Duncan stood in front of the easel in the brightly lit sunroom of the bungalow she shared with her friend Robin. She tilted her head from side to side, staring at it, thinking she wanted to add some birds flying over the turquoise shades of the ocean.

A small boy stood at the water's edge, a pail in his hand. She'd painted glistening diamond-like sparkles where the sun hit the waves. She still needed to add some details. A sandcastle on the beach. Maybe a beach chair and umbrella. She scrunched up her face, trying to decide.

She still wasn't quite used to this style of painting. Very different than the work she'd sold before. Since recently moving back to Belle Island, she'd painted a series of the beach and the small town here on the island, and they were leaning against the wall in a corner of the sunroom as she constantly added to the collection.

Robin entered the room and dropped her bag on the floor. "Hey, you started another painting."

"I did." She was always a bit unsure of showing her work. Especially her new work.

"I still think you should show it to Paul Clark and see if he's interested in doing a showing at his gallery here on the island. Or you could show these new paintings to your agent. It's really great work, Char."

Ha, her agent-slash-boyfriend. She hadn't quite gotten around to telling that whole sorry tale to her friend. "I don't think my work is ready for a showing yet. I'm still working on my style."

"You're too hard on yourself. Always have been. Why not just show Paul a few of your favorites?"

"Maybe. After a bit."

Robin sighed. "You're your own worst critic." She snagged her bag from the floor. "I've got to run. I'm giving Lil lessons on the new software we installed at the inn."

"I'm glad it worked out for you to help manage the inn."

"I love it. Couldn't ask for a better job. I just hope Lil thinks I'm doing a good job. Anyway, I've got to run. Oh, hey, the rent is due. Do you have your check for half? I was going to drop them by the rental office."

"I'll do that today."

"Okay, I'll leave my check on the counter." Robin disappeared out the door with a wave of her hand.

Charlotte put down her paintbrush. Yes, she had money for half the rent. This month. And next. But then she'd have to find a job or sell some of her artwork because that was about all she had left to her name.

Because she'd been a fool.

Ben Hallet stood out on the point in the deepening shadow of the lighthouse. It had been too long. He'd been out of town for longer than he liked, and it was so great to be home. He'd missed the beach, the sunsets, and his friends in the small town on Belle Island. Too many days in the crowded cities with traffic and noise and no opportunity to see the stars. But the travel was part of his job now that he'd taken over running the marina. He went to boat shows, regattas and races, and visited boat manufacturers. He went and checked on the other locations in their chain of marinas. But the part of the job he loved was back on Belle Island at the first marina his father had opened, the main one.

He also needed to call his mom and let her know he was back. She'd been lonely since his father had died. Guilt washed over him that he'd been gone so long. He tried to have dinner with her once a week and dropped by a few other times each week. He'd call tomorrow and catch up with her.

He pushed all those thoughts out of his mind. It was time to just enjoy the beach. This was his regular routine every time he returned to the island from a trip. He'd head straight to the beach. It was almost like the sea breeze stretched out her arms and welcomed him home.

Okay, that was crazy, but he never felt more like he belonged than when he was here on the island. He sank onto the sand, ready to watch the highly anticipated beautiful display of the sunset.

Charlotte walked along the water's edge that evening, headed to Lighthouse Point to watch the sunset. She felt at loose ends these days. Even though she was painting again—thank goodness her 'painter's block' had ended—she still needed to either sell her work or get a job. And what kind of job was she qualified for? All she knew was her art.

She took a deep breath and let the gentle breeze wash away her problems. She rounded the bend and saw a lone person sitting on the beach, looking out to sea. Another sunset watcher. She'd just walk past him and go to the other side of the point. Then they both could have their solitude.

She got closer, ready to just give a brief nod so as not to disturb him.

"Charlotte?"

She paused and looked closely at the man sitting on the beach. "Ben?"

He stood up and gave her a hug. "Wow,

great to see you. It's been years. What, since high school? You here for a visit?"

"I moved back to the island."

"You did? I thought you were in L.A. or something. I heard your work is selling great. Robin is always bragging about you."

If only her work *was* selling...

She plastered on a smile and changed the subject. "So do you still live on the island?"

"I do. I took over the marina."

"Did your dad retire?"

A flash of pain flitted across Ben's face. "No, he died a few years back."

"Oh, no. I didn't know. I'm sorry." She reached out and touched his arm.

"Yeah, it's been tough. Mom is trying to adjust and I'm trying to keep the business going without him, but really, Dad was the business. His skill. His reputation."

"That must be tough."

"It is what it is." Ben shrugged. "So, where are you living now? Your folks moved away a while ago, didn't they?"

"They did. Moved by Eva in Texas. Near Austin."

"How's Eva doing these days?"

She didn't miss the spark in his eyes when he

asked about Eva. She'd always thought that he'd had a crush on her sister when they'd all been growing up here on the island. But then what male hadn't had a crush on her sister? They'd all followed her around, carried her books, bought her shakes at the ice cream shop, and asked her to school dances. She swore her sister had gotten like twenty invites to each school dance… and considering how small their high school had been, that was a good proportion of the guys at the school.

She pushed the thoughts of her sister away and answered, "She's doing fine. I guess. Don't see her much."

"And where are you living now?" Ben swiped the sand from his khaki shorts with a quick brush of his hand. His long, tanned legs reached down to bare feet, and a simple navy t-shirt stretched across his broad shoulders. He exuded a relaxed, I-belong-here attitude. She was envious of that.

"Robin and I got a small bungalow over by the bay."

Ben broke into a grin. "The Bayside Bungalows?"

She nodded.

"That's where I live too. I'm in bungalow

seven. Welcome, neighbor."

"We're in three. I haven't seen you around there, though we've only been there a few weeks."

"I've been out of town. The three of us will have to barbecue out by the bay one night after I get things settled back here at work. I've been away for a while."

"That sounds like a good idea." Charlotte glanced out at the sunset. She'd taken up enough of his time. He probably wanted to just sit with his thoughts, which was what she planned to do. "Well, I should leave you to your sunset watching."

"Why don't you join me, then we'll walk back to the bungalows together?"

She considered the offer and realized it appealed to her much more than sitting and brooding on her problems. "Okay."

He dropped down to the sand again, and she sank beside him, scooping up a handful of sand and letting it trickle through her fingers. The breeze tossed her hair around and she was sorry she hadn't brought something to tie it back.

Ben leaned back on his hands, watching the sky. "Who knew all those years ago in high school that so many of us would end up back on the island? Everyone swore the first thing they were doing after graduation was leaving town."

"Sara is back now, too."

He looked at her with one eyebrow cocked in a questioning glance. "No kidding? Last I heard she was some hotshot at a big ad agency."

"She was, but she moved back to help her aunt at the inn, and now opened her own company here in town."

"A man can't even go out of town on a long business trip these days. The whole town changes." He grinned.

"And she's dating Noah McNeil. Do you know him?"

"Of course. Runs the community center. Moved here quite a while back with his niece. So Sara and Noah are dating, huh?"

"Yes."

"So the inseparable threesome of Sara, Robin, and Charlotte is back together again."

"We are. And that's nice." It had been fun being back here with her friends.

"I'm glad I ran into you to catch up on all the town gossip." He tossed her a smile. "Though, I'm sure there's more. There's *always* more gossip."

"Can't really escape it on Belle Island, can you?" She shrugged. She'd almost forgotten how it was on the island. Everyone knew what everyone else was up to. Knew their neighbors by name. So different from L.A. She'd *maybe* known the name of two people in her huge apartment building back there. It was going to be hard to adjust to small-town life again with everyone knowing her business, but she did like being back here.

They watched while the sun slipped below the horizon, then reflected pink lit up the sky above the clouds. The color slowly darkened into a scarlet-pink slash of color. They both sat in silence, watching the brilliant display. A small sigh escaped her. Sunsets here on the island were almost magical.

Ben finally stood and reached a hand to her. "Guess we should head back before it gets too dark. I still have unpacking to do, but I couldn't miss another sunset."

She took his hand, and he pulled her to her feet. They walked side by side back to Bayside Bungalows, chatting about high school days, as only old friends can do when they see each other after all those years apart.

CHAPTER 2

The next morning, Charlotte clicked off her cell phone and tossed it onto the bed. *Great, just great. Just what she needed.* She sank onto the bed fighting off a feeling of impending doom.

Robin popped her head into the bedroom. "You ready to go?"

"What?" She let out a long, deep breath. "Sure."

"You don't sound so sure. What's wrong?" Robin came in and plopped on the bed beside her. "You don't look very excited about going to the beach. Do you know how long it's been since we've been to the beach?"

"I'm sure it will be fun. It's just that I just got off the phone with my mother. Dad, Mom, and

11

Eva are headed into town. They've booked a cottage at Charming Inn."

Robin raised an eyebrow. "Well, that's… interesting."

Charlotte jumped up and paced the floor. "Interesting. Right. Ha, ha. They haven't been back here in years. Not since they sold our house here and moved to Austin to live near Eva after she got that big-time job there."

Robin leaned back on her elbows, eyeing her. "How long has it been since you've seen them?"

"A couple of years. The last time was a disaster. Christmas two or three years ago."

"Was it still the Eva show?"

Charlotte grinned at her friend's remark. Robin always had a way to make her smile, no matter the predicament. "Pretty much. It was all about Eva's promotion, Eva's boyfriend, Eva this, Eva that."

"So, nothing has changed?"

"Nope. And my father told me I should quit my nonsense life, give up painting, and get a real job."

Robin sat up, wide-eyed. "That's rather cold, even for your father. He does realize you're an adult, right?"

"Doubt it. He doesn't consider a job in the arts a career. He says I should give up my *hobby*. Go back to school for *real* training for a *real* career. The fact that I haven't had a showing of my art in… quite a while… isn't helping to change his mind." She didn't even want to think about how long it had been since she'd had a show. *Ugh.* She sank back down on the bed.

"But you got into that prestigious art school in Paris. You're a talented artist." Robin reached over and squeezed her hand. "Don't let your family get to you. They're crazy-sauce."

She sighed. "I try to ignore their comments, and it's easier to do when they're across the continent. Not so easy if they're coming back to Belle Island. For a week."

"A week? Ouch."

"Seven days, one hundred sixty-eight hours, over 10,000 minutes. But who's counting?"

"Who is?" Robin jumped off the bed and tugged on her hand. "Come on. Let's go to the beach. It will get your mind off of this."

She let herself be pulled off the bed. "You're right. Let's go enjoy ourselves. Then I'll come back and I just need to put my head down and survive their visit."

"When are they coming?"

13

She grabbed her beach bag as they left the bedroom. "Tomorrow…"

Robin and Charlotte headed for the beach. When they arrived, Robin waved to Sara who was already there, setting up a space on the beach. She dropped her bag beside the blanket Sara had spread on the sand. "It's been forever since we've had a beach day."

"I know." Sara nodded. "I've been so busy setting up my new business and you've been busy helping Aunt Lil at the inn."

"We used to come to the beach a couple of times a week, if not more." Robin tugged on the last corner of the blanket, spreading it smooth.

Sara opened a cooler and dug out ice-cold sodas for them. "We've been busy, but I'm glad we made time today."

Charlotte plopped onto the blanket. "And I've been busy… doing nothing."

"Don't say that." Robin shook her head, worried about Charlotte's frame of mind after the call with her mother. Charlotte's parents had always been hard on her. Always compared her to Eva, their golden child, and never recognized

Charlotte's talents. "You've totally redone the two cottages for the inn. They turned out wonderful."

"Aunt Lil loves them," Sara added. "She's still a bit miffed you wouldn't take payment for all the work you did. You should take the money she offered. You know she's going to find a way to pay you anyway. She's almost as hard to win an argument with as Robin is."

Charlotte shrugged. "I enjoyed it. It's not like I was doing much of anything else." She picked up a shell and dragged it through the sand, making a small indentation in the warm white grains.

Sara frowned. "What's up? Where's the real Charlotte? Who is this sad imposter?"

Robin sat down beside Charlotte. "Her folks are coming to town."

"Oh, that's not good." Sara sank down beside them. "When?"

"Tomorrow." It was hard not to miss the forlorn tone of Charlotte's voice.

"How long are they staying?"

"Too long. A week." Robin wrapped her arm around Charlotte's shoulders and gave her a hug. "But we're not going to let them do their usual number on Char this time."

"Right." Sara nodded vigorously, her wavy curls bobbing in the breeze.

Charlotte looked out at the water. "I just want to click my ruby slippers and have the week be over."

"How about if Sara and I run interference?"

Charlotte looked doubtful. "I'm not sure if that will work. You know my parents. They are pretty persistent with their opinions."

"Wait until they see your new work. These new paintings are fabulous." Sara handed a soda to Charlotte.

Charlotte popped it open and took a sip. "I'm not sure nostalgic paintings are really something that would impress my father."

"Hmph. We don't care what your father thinks. They are wonderful. Emotional." Robin held a hand up against the bright sun rays and looked out to the water. "I think what we need is a dip in the ocean." She jumped up, tugging on Charlotte's hand.

Sara jumped up, too. "Race you."

With that, the three of them raced to the water, leaping into the waves, splashing each other and laughing. Just like they'd done when they were young girls.

Robin watched as Charlotte relaxed as they

goofed around in the water. It was pretty hard to stay stressed out when playing in the waves with your two best friends.

Ben walked in the back door to the kitchen at Charming Inn. Jay stood by the oven, pulling out a tray of something that smelled delicious. He was wearing one of his ever-present t-shirts with a slogan. *Life Begins After Coffee.* Ben would have to agree with that one.

"Whatcha got there?"

"Cookies. I made my secret recipe sugar cookies." He nodded to a batch cooling on a wire rack.

"Which you'll share with your best friend, right?" Ben reached over and swiped a cookie.

Jay rolled his eyes. "But, of course. Gotta feed the starving bachelor."

Ben leaned against the counter, munching the warm cookie. "These are the best sugar cookies ever."

"That's what my grandma always said."

"So why are yours better than anyone else's?"

"If I told you my secret…"

"I know, I know… you'd have to kill me."

"No, I was going to say if I told you my secret my grandmother would kill *me*."

He laughed. "Well, we don't want you killed because where would the inn be without their famous chef?"

"I'm not sure I'm quite famous."

"You don't think the crowds that come to the inn for meals are coming for the view, do you? You can get a great view all over the island."

Jay shrugged off the compliment. "So, how was your business trip?"

"It was too long to be on the road. Glad to be home."

Jay slid the cookies from the baking sheet to the cooling rack. "Back to pester me and steal cookies."

"Yep."

He and Jay turned at the sound of someone entering the kitchen.

"Hey, Lil." Jay greeted the owner of the inn. "Ben here is eating into your profits."

Lil Charm beamed a welcoming smile. "Ben's always welcome to sample your wares, especially after he got us such a good deal on the boat we finally got to replace our old one."

"Ha, see? Lil loves me." He swiped another cookie. "Hated to see your old boat go. She was a beauty, but I'm afraid repairs to her were going to keep getting more and more expensive."

"We love the used boat you found for us. I do like a nice cruise around the bay."

He munched on his second stolen cookie.

"I'm gonna ban you from my kitchen if you keep that up." Jay waved a spatula.

"I just came in to say the girls are going to all be eating here tonight in the dining room. They're at the beach having a girls' day and I suggested they end it with dinner here."

"I heard Sara moved back here." Ben eyed the cookies, wondering if he could swipe another one when Jay wasn't looking.

"Sara came here when I had my fall." Lil tapped her cane on the floor. "I'm about ready to lose this silly cane though."

"Not quite yet." Jay frowned.

"Soon," Lil countered.

Jay set the cookie sheet into the large stainless sink and grabbed a cookie himself. "And Charlotte and Robin moved into a place at Bayside Bungalows."

"I know, I ran into Charlotte last night at

19

Lighthouse Point. Hadn't seen her or Sara in years."

Robin, Charlotte, and Sara. The dynamic trio. They'd been inseparable when he'd gone to school with them. They'd all hung out in the same group of kids in high school—though that had been over twenty years ago—then everyone had drifted apart, going to college or moving away for jobs. It was good to see the three girls, at least, were still close friends.

"I better run. I promised Mom I'd stop by. No offense to your cooking, Jay, but she wants to take me to Magic Cafe, and I never turn down a free meal."

"You want to meet me later at Lucky Duck for a beer?"

"Sure. Sounds great." He turned to Lil. "Glad to see you're up and doing well."

"Don't encourage her. She'll throw her cane away." Jay shook his head.

"It would already be gone if you and Sara didn't nag me all the time."

"I'm outta here. I'll let you two sort that out." He slipped out the back door and headed down the sidewalk.

After a quick five-minute walk, he was at his childhood home. He climbed the familiar steps up to the back door and opened it. His mother turned at the sound of him entering and a wide smile spread across her face. She hurried over and gave him a big hug. He wrapped his arms around her.

"I'm so glad to see you." She stepped back and looked him over from top to bottom as if checking to make sure he was okay.

He grinned. "I'm fine, Mom. And really glad to be home."

"It seems like forever since I've seen you."

"Well, I'm back now. And you're treating me to Magic Cafe. What more could a man ask for?"

"You probably have better things to do than spend the evening with your mother."

He shook his head. "Not that I can think of."

"Let me just finish up these dishes. Will only take a minute. I do hate to come back to a messy kitchen."

He lounged against the counter while his mother finished her chores. "Why don't you come by the marina tomorrow? There's a really nice new yacht we're working on."

"I don't think I can. I'm pretty busy tomorrow."

His mother was never busy. She just didn't like coming to the marina much anymore after his father had died. She used to work in the front office occasionally and handle some of the paperwork, but that had all stopped.

He wished he could convince her to get out of the house more. He was worried about her. The extent of her outings each week was a trip or two to the grocery store and church on Sunday. She'd pulled back from the couples she and his dad had been friends with, unwilling to go to things alone.

"Okay, I'm ready now." She put down her dish towel and grabbed her purse.

They walked outside, and she carefully locked her door. He helped her into her years-old but still serviceable car and drove to Magic Cafe, hoping to have a nice dinner and make her smile and laugh. She used to always laugh. Sing in the kitchen. Walk all over the island.

He darted a look at her. She was staring out her window, watching the scenery. His mother was much too young to be this... old.

CHAPTER 3

"Hey, Willie." Ben slid onto a barstool at Lucky Duck after dinner with his mom.

"Ben, back in town, I see. The usual?"

Ben nodded. Willie grabbed a cold mug and filled it with a local craft beer. Ben had missed that, too. His favorite beer, sitting here at Lucky Duck, hanging out with Jay.

He'd had a nice dinner with his mom at Magic Cafe, then taken her back to her house. The house was really too big for her now. It was the house he'd been raised in, and his mom just rattled around in the four-bedroom house, all alone. He'd tried to convince her to move into something smaller, or even move to the new retirement community on the island. She had some friends who had moved there. Or people he used to consider her friends before she'd become the hermit she was now.

But she wasn't ready to give up that house and all the memories it held. It was directly on the beach, and she did love to sit out there with her morning coffee and watch the world awaken. He'd taken over doing most of the repairs around the house and helped out when he could. She was still part owner of the marina, so she had that income coming in plus his father's life insurance money, so it wasn't like she *had* to downsize. He just worried about her living there all alone.

He took a swig of the beer. "Thanks, Willie."

"You bet." Willie turned to greet another customer.

Ben looked around the room, waved to a few people he knew, and turned back to the bar. Before long Jay slid onto the stool beside him.

Willie brought Jay the same local beer. "So, how was dinner with your mom?"

"Fine. She's glad I'm back. Lonely, I think."

"You should see if she'd join one of the groups at the community center."

"I should. Not sure what kind of groups they have going there, though."

24

Jay nodded at a group of people coming into the tavern. "There's Noah. You could ask him."

Jay's expression changed, his eyes lighting up, as Robin, Sara, and Charlotte entered with Noah. Ben shook his head, wondering if his friend was ever going to ask Robin out. He waved to the group and they headed over.

He jumped off his seat and gave Sara a hug. "I hear you're back in town."

"I am."

"Want to join us? Why don't we all grab a table? That work for everyone? I'd love to catch up with you."

They moved to a table in the corner of the bar and Ben didn't miss that Jay ended up sitting next to Robin. Sara and Noah sat beside each other, their hands resting together on the table. Charlotte took a seat beside Ben.

Willie sent a waitress over for drink orders. Soon they were talking about high school escapades and whatever happened to this person or that person. Jay and Noah were a bit left out on the high school reminiscences but sat and listened to the stories.

Ben finally turned to Noah. "So... I'm hoping to get my mom out of the house more.

Maybe she could join one of the groups at the community center?"

"What does your mom like to do?"

"She…" What did she like to do? It seemed like her whole life had been about raising him and his brother and taking care of his father. "She… knits? Likes to read?"

"We have a monthly book club, and there's an active knitter's group that meets up a couple mornings a week for coffee and knitting."

"Maybe I can convince her to join one of those."

"I'll see if I can get one of the members of those groups to call her and invite her," Noah suggested.

"That would be great." If he could just get her involved in something. She'd had time to grieve, and he knew she'd never get over losing his dad, but she still had so much life to live. He wanted her to have the best one possible.

He turned to Charlotte. "So did you girls have dinner at the inn?"

"We did. We officially decided we had the best day ever. We haven't had a girls' day like that in forever."

Her blue eyes shone. He remembered when they were studying genetics in high school and they'd learned how rare it was to have red hair and blue eyes. Charlotte had been a high school celebrity in that class.

"So are you still painting?"

"I am. I've just… I don't know how to describe it… changed my technique some since I've moved back here. I've been painting beach scenes and a few of downtown Main Street."

"I'd love to see them."

"Oh, they're not really ready to be seen. I'm still working on them. It's so different than what I did before."

He could hear the uncertainty in her voice. She'd never been very secure in her belief in herself, he remembered that. But then she'd lived in the shadow of her ever-so-popular, one-year-older sister.

Robin leaned closer. "Her work now is fabulous. Don't let her tell you otherwise. I want her to show them to Paul Clark."

"That's a great idea." He nodded.

"They aren't ready." Charlotte's words left no room for debate.

Not that that would stop Robin. "I'm right though. You should show them to him."

Ben grinned. Hard to win an argument with Robin. Everyone in town knew that.

"I should probably call it a night. My family's coming to town tomorrow and—" Charlotte shrugged. And what? She needed a good night's sleep to face them? Maybe she could sleep through their entire visit…

"I'll go, too." Robin stood.

"No, you don't have to leave. Stay and have fun."

Ben stood. "I'm beat. I'll walk back with you. You know, now that we're neighbors."

Robin sat back down by Jay. "Okay. I won't be long, though."

Charlotte and Ben headed outside and walked down Oak Street. They crossed over to the gazebo and headed down the bay side of the island. As they walked, Ben kept looking up at the sky.

"What are you looking for up there? A shooting star?"

"Nah, I just like seeing the stars. We're lucky here on the island, aren't we?"

"We are." Well, she had been until she heard her family was coming to town.

"So your family is coming to visit?"

"Yes." She knew her voice didn't hold even a tiny bit of enthusiasm.

He stopped and looked at her. "Things still rocky with your family?"

She frowned. "How did you know things were strained?"

He shrugged. "It was hard to miss some of your parents' comments when we were younger. They were pretty hard on you."

"Let's just say things haven't changed much."

"Eva coming in, too?"

"Sure is." Ben would probably be happy with that. Everyone on Belle Island would be glad to see Eva. She was that person.

"I'll have to see if I can catch up with her, too, then."

Of course, he would. He'd probably be one of a long line of admirers holding onto Eva's every word. "Yeah, you should do that." Once again, not much enthusiasm in her voice.

They continued their walk in silence.

"Well, here's my bungalow," she said.

"It was fun tonight. We should do it again." Ben stood by her front door.

"Sure." He'd probably be too busy chasing down Eva. "Night, Ben."

"Night."

He crossed the courtyard and entered his cottage, and then she slipped inside and headed for her room. She kicked off her shoes and flopped on the bed, staring at the ceiling. This pity party she was throwing wasn't really her thing... but she really, *really* was *not* looking forward to her family's week-long visit.

CHAPTER 4

Sara stood by the reception desk at the inn. Her Aunt Lil was not listening to reason. "You should take it easy. You've been up since dawn and you've been on your feet for far too long. You don't want to overdo it."

"You don't want to tell me what to do, now do you?" Aunt Lil raised an eyebrow.

"I just worry about you."

"Well, don't. I'm healing just fine."

Sara looked around behind the reception counter. "Where's your cane?"

"I must have left it in my office."

"But—"

"Sara, that's enough. I'm fine. Quit treating me like an invalid."

She sighed. "I'm sorry. I don't mean to do that."

"Don't you have work to do?" Aunt Lil asked pointedly.

"I do. I was just headed out to look at some rental property on Oak Street. A small office space. The rent isn't much, and at least I'd have an office for the business. I know I've kind of just taken over The Nest." She adored the private area of the inn that they'd dubbed The Nest years ago when Aunt Lil had become her guardian after her parents died.

"Then, you should run along and look at it instead of worrying about me."

She turned when she heard a group of people approaching.

"Sara, how good to see you. It's been a long time" Charlotte's sister, Eva, flashed her a charming smile. She still was beautiful. Maybe more beautiful as she aged. How did some women do that?

"Hi, Eva. Hi, Mr. and Mrs. Duncan."

"Sara, dear, are you back visiting, too?" Mrs. Duncan looked at her as if evaluating her to see how much she'd changed.

Sara wasn't sure if she'd passed inspection or not. "I've moved back to the island."

"Really?" Mrs. Duncan's look showed clear disapproval. "So, both you and Charlotte have returned? Though, I'm sure Charlotte isn't planning on staying long. I mean, what is there for her to *do* here?"

"Paint?" Sara stated the obvious.

"No, Isadora means there isn't anything for her to do here to earn a living." Mr. Duncan cut in.

Before she could say something she shouldn't, Aunt Lil came to the rescue. "Let's get you all checked in, shall we?" Aunt Lil turned to her. "Go along and look at your rental space. I've got everything here covered."

Sara backed away and let her aunt deal with Charlotte's family. Poor Char. It was going to be a long, long week…

She paused on the front porch and pulled her phone out and texted Charlotte.

They're here. Good luck. Let me know if I can run interference for you or if you just need to vent.

That afternoon Noah popped into Belle Island Inn, another inn on the island owned by Susan and her son, Jamie. He loved the comfortable atmosphere and knew it attracted quite a crowd during busy season. They'd recently branched into becoming a popular wedding venue, too.

He wanted to see if Dorothy was working the front desk. If anyone could convince Ben's mother to join the knitting group, it was Dorothy.

He was in luck. She was working. He waited until she checked in a customer, then walked up to the desk. "Dorothy, I wondered if you could do me a big favor."

"Sure, Noah. What do you need?"

"You know Ruby Hallet, right?"

"Sure do. Ran into her at the market just the other day."

"Her son, Ben, is hoping she'll get out more. He wants to see if he can get her interested in joining some groups."

"I know she's been struggling since she lost her husband, but justifiably so." Dorothy's kind eyes shone with understanding.

"Ben told me she's a knitter. I thought that maybe if you personally invited her, she'd come to your knitting group at the community center."

"That's a great idea. We'd love to have her. I

should have thought of that myself." Dorothy nodded vigorously. "I'll make it a point to drop by to see her and invite her."

"That would be great. I'm hoping if she joins the knitting group, maybe she'll join the book club too. Ben said she's a big reader."

"I will say, Noah, you've done great things with our community center. So many groups and activities."

"Thanks. I admit, I really love my job there."

A couple came up to the desk, so he turned to leave. "Thanks, Dorothy. Hope you have success with Ruby."

He left and headed back to the community center. Well, he'd at least done that much to help Ruby. He always felt his job extended to even more than just the community center... it widened to helping all the people of Belle Island. The island had been very good to him, and he planned to repay her in any way he could.

Charlotte trudged over to Charming Inn, each step taking more and more effort. Her sister had texted to say they'd arrived. A text that came in two hours after Sara's text, not that she minded the reprieve. Her family was evidently in no hurry to see her...

She'd agreed to come to the inn for drinks and dinner, though she was not looking forward to it. She often imagined what it would be like to have a close family. One filled with laughter and family jokes and automatic acceptance. Maybe that type of family was really just some kind of fairy tale.

She stood in front of the deck to the inn, gathering her courage. Sara popped out the front door. "I was stalking you on the Buddies app. Saw you were here."

"I'm here."

Sara laughed. "Don't sound so enthusiastic."

She sucked in a deep breath of air. "I'll be fine."

"Just a warning. Your mom is of the mindset that your move here is just a temporary visit."

"Of course she is. Even though I told them I've moved here and it's my permanent home base now."

"They're worried about you finding work here. I told them you were painting."

"Which isn't a real job to them." And, to be

honest, wasn't paying much now. She did have to find something to bring in some money. And soon. "I better go in and see them."

"You'll be fine. Don't let them get to you." Sara hugged her, and she took strength in her friend's embrace.

"Easier said than done." She walked up the steps with Sara at her side and entered the inn.

"They're out on the deck, having drinks. They have a reservation for dinner in forty-five minutes." Sara nodded toward the deck.

Forty-five minutes of happy hour. She could do that, right? She squared her shoulders and crossed over to the door to the deck, pasting on a smile that she hoped was a confident, self-assured one. She stepped through the doorway.

Her mother waved from a grouping of chairs across the deck. She waved back and crossed the distance.

Her father stood and shook her hand. "Good to see you."

Eva motioned to the empty chair beside her. "Sit."

More a command than an offer…

"I've ordered you Chardonnay." Her mother motioned to a glass of white wine sitting on the table in front of the chairs.

She didn't like Chardonnay. And her mother knew that. But her mother was certain it was the drink of choice at the beach.

Okay, then. She sank onto the chair beside Eva. Her sister was dressed in a tailored sleeveless dress and fancy sandals that probably cost more than her monthly rent at the bungalow. Her mother was also precisely dressed... way overdressed for a relaxed beach inn dinner. Her father had on neatly pressed slacks and a long-sleeved button-down shirt. They looked more like they were going to the country club than dinner at the inn.

She looked down at her flowy skirt, simple white t-shirt, and worn but ever-so-comfortable sandals. She might as well have been going to a different dinner than her family. She eyed the white wine, wondering if she could stand to take a sip or two, and hoping she could order red wine, or a beer, or a stronger drink at dinner.

"We'd so hoped to stay at Belle Island Inn this visit—it's such a classic inn—but can you believe it was full? I guess Susan and her son have really brought things around in the last few years. It was never full when her brother ran it. Anyway, we did find a cottage available here at

Charming Inn. It's… okay." Her mother gave a small shrug.

She bit her tongue, wanting to spit out that Charming Inn was wonderful and, well, *charming*. But she stayed silent. She'd learned long ago it was better not to disagree with anything her mother said. Belle Island Inn was lovely, but Charming Inn and Cottages held a special place in her heart. It was where she'd spent hours and hours growing up, always accepted by Lil, always welcome.

"We're staying in the Teal Cottage. Like a color is good for a cottage name?" Eva laughed. "We wanted the large four-bedroom cottage, but it wasn't available. We're in a tiny two-bedroom cottage and it's very cramped. Who knew this island would become so… crowded. I hope it's not too touristy now."

She knew for a fact the teal cottage was spacious and airy. And she guessed she wouldn't mention that she was the one who'd decorated it.

"So, what have you been up to since you got here?" Her father leaned back in his chair.

"Doing some work. Painting."

"Have you looked for a job yet?" He eyed her over his glass of scotch.

She considered what her best option was here. She could say she was busy painting—which she was—or say she was looking for a job just to keep them happy. Before she could answer, Lil came out on the deck and walked over to them.

She held out a glass of red wine to Charlotte. "Here, try this. I always value your opinion on red wine. It's a new one I'm thinking of adding to the menu." Lil turned and smiled graciously at her mother and father. "Charlotte is quite the help around here. She jumped in when I was a bit indisposed and helped with the remodeling of two of our cottages. Painting, picking out furniture and painting it. They turned out lovely. Your daughter is very talented."

Please don't tell them I did the teal cottage. She sent thoughts winging over to Lil. The last thing she needed was her family to critique her work on that cottage. Which *she* thought turned out darling.

And she could have jumped up and hugged Lil for her support, but instead, she accepted the offered red wine and took a sip. "Oh, this is very nice. A hint of black cherry, but still very dry. I like it."

Lil beamed. "Good, that's what I thought. I think I'll add it to our wine list." Lil turned and waved at some other customers sitting across the deck. "I better go say hi to Julie and Reed. I can't believe Reed talked Julie into taking the night off. You remember Julie, don't you? She owns The Sweet Shoppe here in town."

"Vaguely." Her mother shrugged that dismissive shrug that Charlotte was beginning to get annoyed at.

Nice, Mom. Really nice.

"Of course you do," Charlotte said. "She makes those wonderful blueberry muffins and pecan pie and... well, lots of great things." She didn't know why she had to defend the people of Belle Island to her mother, but she did.

"Mother and I don't eat many sweets." Eva took a dainty sip of her white wine.

Fine, the more for me. She pasted on a fake smile and looked at her watch. How long could this happy hour go on?

"Well, enjoy your dinner." Lil smiled and walked over to Julie and Reed.

Charlotte looked longingly after her, wishing she could escape over to the other side of the deck, plop down by Julie, and have a nice chat.

41

About muffins, or pies, or the weather. She didn't care. Just over *there* and not over *here*.

"I heard the dining room here has expanded and they have a new cook, thank goodness. Do you think the food is any good?" her mother asked with a bit of a scowl on her face.

"It's delicious." She clasped the end of the armrest.

"I hope it's passable. Though we can go to Magic Cafe, of course. The view is nice there, too and the food is okay." Eva set her drink on the table.

Charlotte looked from her father, to her mother, to her sister. Who were these people? Such snobs. So negative. If they weren't family, she'd never have them in her life. How could she be from the same genes?

She stood. "Let's go see if our table is ready." She grabbed her red wine and left the white wine sitting on the table on the deck.

CHAPTER 5

B en looked up from his table where he was contemplating ordering some of Jay's chicken-fried steak. He still hadn't gotten around to grocery shopping since he'd been back, so he'd headed to the inn for dinner.

Charlotte walked in the room with her family. Eva was striking, as always. She seemed to sweep the attention of the customers toward her as she entered. Charlotte looked... pale.

He watched while the Duncans made their way to a table by the window with a great view of the gulf. Mr. Duncan held out a chair for his wife, then Eva. Charlotte sank into her own chair, unassisted.

He remembered that Charlotte's parents had always favored Eva. That fact had been obvious to everyone in town. Charlotte looked a bit beaten down tonight. Without really thinking, he jumped up and crossed over to their table.

"Hi." He stood beside their table.

"Ben Hallet. How are you?" Eva gave him her famous dazzling smile.

He didn't let it affect him. Much.

"Ah, Ben. How are you?" Mr. Duncan reached out and shook his hand.

"I'm doing fine, thanks."

Mrs. Duncan seemed to be busy with her menu.

"I heard you were coming to town to visit Charlotte." He glanced at Charlotte and smiled. She sent him a weak smile in return.

"Oh, it's not really to visit Charlotte. We just decided Belle Island would be a nice place to vacation since we used to live here," Eva said.

He blinked, not sure he'd heard correctly. "Oh… ah…"

Charlotte sent him a warning look.

"Well, we're sure glad that Char moved back to the island," he insisted.

"Char*lotte* is only here for a visit." Mrs. Duncan finally looked up from the menu.

"Oh, I thought it was a permanent move.

You know, as permanent as anything is these days."

"Temporary." Mr. Duncan nodded. "So, would you like to join us, son?"

Mrs. Duncan sent her husband a glare, which cinched the decision for him.

"Love to." He slipped into the seat beside Charlotte. She looked at him in surprise. "I was just getting ready to order Jay's chicken-fried steak."

Eva scrunched up her nose. "Really? That's... an interesting choice."

"Best on the island."

Charlotte was glad for the interference from Ben, but was he crazy? Why would he volunteer to have dinner with her family?

"I think I'll have the chicken-fried steak, too," she said in solidarity.

"Fish is better for you," her mother said pointedly.

"But the chicken-fried steak sounds delicious." She set down her menu, hoping to end the discussion.

They placed their orders and sat chatting about the weather. Okay, that was safe.

"So, Ben, what do you do these days?" her mother asked.

"I've taken over my father's business."

"Oh, you're a boat mechanic?" Eva asked.

Charlotte glared at her sister. "No, he owns a chain of marinas up and down the coast."

Ben leaned back in his chair, unaffected by Eva's remark. "I do some repairs. Dad taught me everything I know about boats."

"Well, isn't that interesting?" her mother asked without a bit of sincerity.

"I'm sure it's a big responsibility running all of that." Charlotte nodded at Ben, hoping he didn't just up and leave her alone with her family.

"It is. Didn't expect to run it this soon, but after Dad got sick... well, it fell to me to take over."

"We should talk about something more cheerful." Eva interrupted the conversation. "Do you have any boats we could go out on? I haven't boated since we moved away."

"We have a few." Ben didn't even blink at the change of conversation.

"So, would you take me out boating?" Eva batted her eyes at Ben.

Seriously? Batting her eyes?

As expected, Ben fell under her spell. "I think I could work out something."

"Perfect. Maybe we could all boat out to Blue Heron Island?" Eva sent Ben one of her famous smiles that seemed to make all men do her bidding.

"I'm sure Ben is busy working. He just got back in town." She gave him an out.

"No, I can fit it in this week. We'll make a day of it. A picnic out to Blue Heron Island. How does that sound? I'll get Jay to make us up a picnic lunch."

"Perfect." Eva clapped her hands and smiled, pleased she'd gotten her way.

Of course, she'd gotten her way. She always did. With a flip of her blonde hair—that never seemed to lose its perfect curls—and a flash of her dazzling smile, the world parted for her and did as she commanded.

Eva turned to her. "You'll come with us, right?"

More of a statement again, rather than a question. So, she was going to be included?

"I can probably make time."

"You aren't really doing anything now, are you?" Her mother did one of her so-irritating dismissive shrugs.

"I've been busy painting," she insisted.

"Right. So you're not busy." Eva added.

Charlotte reached for her red wine and decided the best course of action to get through the meal was to just keep quiet.

Keep quiet and sip red wine.

CHAPTER 6

Charlotte escaped as soon as possible after their dinner was over, begging off with a headache she didn't really have.

She walked out onto the wide front porch of the inn and took in a deep breath, trying to steady her nerves and wash away all memory of tonight's dinner. Well, that was one day down of her family's trip to town. Only six more to go.

"Char?"

She turned at the sound of her name. "Hey, Sara."

"I've been hanging around, waiting for your dinner to finish. I wanted to see how it went."

"About as expected. I was told a litany of things I'm doing wrong, jobs I should go after, and, well, my clothing choices could be better."

49

"Oh, Char, I'm sorry."

"I'm used to it. And Eva sat there charming Ben with her stories. I swear every man in the dining room under ninety was staring at her. Heck, even men *over* ninety stare at her."

Sara scowled. "I could throw out a trite saying like 'beauty is only skin deep,' but I won't. I'll just say that you are a beautiful, talented person. Don't let your family do a number on you."

"Thanks, it's nice to hear some compliments…"

"Why don't we go to The Nest and have a drink?"

"I think I'll just head home. That whole dinner and drink ordeal just made me tired."

"You sure?"

"I'm sure."

"Okay, but I'm going to check on you again tomorrow."

She flashed her friend a weak smile. "I'll be fine." She climbed down the last steps from the porch and headed back to her bungalow. The one where there wasn't any family or constant criticism.

She slowly walked along the sidewalk until she heard someone call her name.

"Char, wait up." Ben jogged up to her.

"I thought you'd be catching a nightcap with Eva."

"Nah, I've got an early morning."

She looked at him, surprised the responsibility could trump Eva's flirty words and dazzling smile. He fell into step beside her as they leisurely strolled to Bayside Bungalows.

"So, your family… they are… how do I put this?" He paused his steps, and she stopped beside him. "You and Eva are different."

She choked out a laugh. "You could say that. She is beautiful and the shining star in my parents' lives."

He stared at her for a long moment, then frowned. "But you're beautiful, too. And kind, and talented."

"Did Sara put you up to this pep talk?" She cocked her head to the side, searching his face.

"What? No. I meant every word."

"I'm not the dazzling beauty that Eva is. Always perfectly dressed. And I swear, I have no idea how she keeps her hair looking so perfect. Never out of place." She swept her own coppery hair behind her shoulders. It was always flying this way and that in its own mischievous way. "She's got a dream job making big bucks. She's everything a parent could want in a child."

"They must be proud of you, too. You're a talented painter."

"No, I got lucky and sold some of my work. Had my moment of semi-fame in the art world. I seemed to have fizzled out."

"I heard your new work is great."

"Says my best friends, not art critics."

"Why don't you show it to Paul Clark? See what he says?"

"I wish everyone would stop suggesting that. I'm not ready." She turned and started walking away.

He jogged to catch up with her again. "I'm sorry. You're right. It's your decision. I didn't mean to make you mad."

She stopped and turned to him. "No, I'm sorry. I'm just... cranky. My family does that to me. You'd best just make a wide berth around me this week until my family leaves. Oh, and then give me more time to get over them." She grinned. "And maybe some more time after that."

"I'm sorry you're having such a tough time with them here."

She saw genuine sympathy in his eyes. But

she didn't want sympathy. She just wanted… What did she want? She had no clue anymore.

"Let's just go back to our bungalows and leave all talk of my family behind us."

"Sounds like a plan." Ben dropped into step beside her and they silently walked down the sidewalk then cut across to the bay and their bungalows.

"Good night, Ben." She climbed the steps to her front door.

"Sweet dreams, Char."

Sweet dreams. Ha. She'd probably have dreams of failure all night. Or wearing her pajamas to a formal party. Or her hair looking like she'd stuck her finger in a light socket.

Ben took a few steps, then turned back around. "You know, it isn't any of my business, but—"

"But you're going to say it anyway, right?"

He grinned. "Right." He took the few steps back to stand beside her. "The only person who needs to be proud of you is you. If you believe in yourself, it doesn't matter what anyone else thinks."

She watched as he walked away, across the courtyard. He was right, of course. The only thing was, she had no idea how to make that happen. Too many years of being told she was falling short. And then her art career had folded. She had almost no money left.

It was incredibly hard to believe in herself with all of that hanging over her head.

Ben crossed to his cottage and opened the door. He took one last look back toward Charlotte. She was still standing on her front porch, lost in thought. He hoped she'd listened to his words. Her family was hard on her. Dismissive. He couldn't imagine that. His parents had always been his biggest supporters and his mother still was.

He walked inside and dropped his keys on the table. Charlotte was right. Eva was a looker. Beautiful. And Eva knew it and used it. He was certain that Eva had learned to use her looks to get where she wanted with her job and in life, not caring who she stepped on in the process.

Oh, he admitted he'd had a schoolboy crush on her when they where young. Who hadn't? But then as they all got older, he'd realized she wasn't really the kind of girl he wanted. Not that he hadn't still fallen under her spell now and again when she'd asked him for a favor, like "helping" her write her English essay, or taking her and her friends out on his father's boat.

Well, he *still* fell under her spell, despite himself. He was taking them all out to Blue Heron Island even though his week was more than packed with work at the marina. He shook his head. He was weak.

He walked over to a shelf and plucked off a photograph of a group of friends from high school. Charlotte stood at the edge of the group, her hair flying in the breeze, a genuine smile on her face. She didn't seem to realize it, but she was beautiful. In a different way than Eva, but beautiful all the same. A genuine beauty that was more than just her looks. It was the way she was with people. An aura of friendship and acceptance surrounded her.

He set the photo back on the shelf, determined to help Charlotte get through this week with her family. And after that, who knew?

CHAPTER 7

C harlotte woke to the sun streaming through her window. She rolled over and looked at her clock. Nine o'clock. Which in L.A. she'd have considered an ungodly hour of the morning, but she'd gotten so she actually liked the mornings here on Belle Island. She stretched, climbed out of bed, and headed to the kitchen for coffee.

Robin had left her a note. *Headed to work at the inn. Come by and tell me how yesterday went.*

She poured herself a cup of coffee and sank into a kitchen chair. Yesterday had been a disaster. But, in the light of day, she knew that some of that had been her own making. She'd let the things her family said get to her. She hadn't stood up for herself. She and her family did the same dance over and over again.

And she let them.

She took a sip of the coffee. Maybe some of the words Ben had said had seeped into her brain overnight.

If she didn't change how she reacted, nothing would change. Nothing.

She jumped up, grabbed the coffee, and headed for the shower.

Today things would change. She'd stand up to them. Tell them that art was her life. Tell them...

She didn't know what all she'd tell them, but she was tired of the poor-Char stage of her life.

That changed today.

When she got out of the shower, she saw she had a text from Eva.

We're having lunch at Magic Cafe. One o'clock. Meet us there.

Okay, she would meet them there. And she'd talk to them. Explain things. And they could either accept her as she was or not. Their choice. Determination surged through her. It was time things changed with her family. New dynamics.

She pulled on a t-shirt and old shorts. She still had time to paint for an hour or so before heading out to Magic Cafe. She was in the middle of painting a nighttime scene of the gazebo at the end of Oak Street. Lamps glowed on the brick pathway circling the gazebo where a young couple sat, their foreheads touching.

She wanted to add a full moon up in the sky and a silvery moonlight surrounding the scene. She picked up her paintbrush and started to work.

CHAPTER 8

"Charlotte is always late." Eva looked around Magic Cafe. "I can't believe she'd keep us waiting like this. It's hot here, and I'd like to order." She fanned herself with her menu.

"Let's give her a few more minutes." Her father took a sip of his drink, obviously in no hurry. But then he never seemed to mind the heat.

She never had liked the heat and humidity of Florida. The ceiling fans above them on the outside area moved the air, but she would have preferred to sit inside in the air-conditioned area. Her father had insisted on sitting outside with the expansive view of the water and she hadn't been able to make him change his mind.

Annoyed, she took a sip of her iced tea and fanned herself again. She looked over as a couple came out to the outside dining area and clapped her hands in glee. "Oh, look. It's Camille." She jumped up and waved.

Camille and her date threaded their way over to the table. Camille gave her a quick kiss on both cheeks. "Eva, darling, it's been forever. What are you doing here?"

"We decided to take a quick vacation back here on the island."

"I'm so glad you did. We're here for a little visit ourselves." She turned to the man beside her. "I want you to meet Delbert. Delbert Hamilton of Hamilton Hotels."

Her father stood and shook the man's hand. "I'm Glen Duncan. Nice to meet you, Mr. Hamilton."

"Please, call me Del."

"Del it is. And this is my wife, Isadora, and my daughter who's been chatting away with Camille is Eva."

Del nodded to all of them. "Nice to meet you."

"Would you like to join us? We could get Tally to move us to a larger table. Say yes. I'd

love to catch up with what you've been doing."
She motioned to a large table nearby.

"Delbert, honey, is it okay if we join the Duncans?"

"Of course." Delbert lifted a hand to wave to Tally. "Tally, I hate to bother you, but do you think we could all move to a larger table?"

"Of course, let me just get one set up. It's not a problem."

They all moved to the new, larger table and Delbert and Camille ordered drinks.

"We're waiting on my sister, Charlotte. She's late." Eva looked at Delbert. "The girl has no sense of time." She rolled her eyes.

Just then Charlotte walked up to the table, looking surprised at the enlarged group. "Camille, uh... hi." She looked at Delbert.

"This is Delbert Hamilton," Eva said. "We invited Camille and Del to join us. And you're late."

"I'm sorry. I was painting and lost track of time."

"It always pays to be punctual," her mother chimed in.

It did pay to be punctual. How did her sister manage to go through life in such a haphazard

63

way? Her whole free-spirited artist type was just… annoying.

Charlotte had talked to herself the whole way over to Magic Cafe, not rushing even though she knew she was late and would hear about her tardiness. She'd rehearsed the words she was going to say to her family, over and over and over. What she hadn't expected was Camille and her boyfriend to be at the table. Now was not the time to have a serious talk with her family. She slipped into her chair beside Delbert and smiled at him.

Camille leaned forward. "Delbert is Delbert Hamilton of Hamilton Hotels."

"Oh." What did one say to an introduction like that? She'd, of course, heard of Hamilton Hotels.

He smiled back at her. "We recently purchased a hotel in Sarasota and remodeled it into a Hamilton Hotel. So I'm here on the island quite a bit while that's all going on. It's a bit different than our regular hotels and I'm quite proud of how it turned out."

"Delbert is making a name for himself in

the hotel business, but I do quite like his father's more formal hotels." Camille rested her hand on his arm.

"That's nice." *Where was the waitress?* She wanted to order a beer. The server came over and she did just that, much to her mother's displeasure and annoying dismissive shrug.

"Eva, dear, you must, *must* come to a party Mama's throwing this week. Everyone will be there. Senators. The Governor. Some state representatives from Mississippi will be there, too. You know how it is when Mama throws a party. Just *everyone* wants to be invited." She turned and added. "Oh, and Mr. and Mrs. Duncan, you should come, too."

"We'd love to, dear," her mother said.

Charlotte sat there, invisible.

"And, of course, Charlotte, you should come, too," Delbert added.

Nothing like being an afterthought.

"Thank you. I'll check my calendar." Not that they'd even said what day it was. She was pretty sure she was going to be so very busy that night, though.

"The attire is casual." Camille looked at Charlotte's outfit with a look of disapproval. "Well, you know, Mama's version of casual. A *nice* dress and the men will all be wearing slacks and dress shirts, I'm sure."

Charlotte smiled at the waitress bringing her beer, reached for it, and took a long swallow.

Ice cold. Nice.

Eva and Camille chattered away through the entire meal, talking about clothes and celebrities and television shows she'd never even heard of. She rarely watched TV. She was more of a reader if she had free time.

She sat quietly, concentrating on her grouper sandwich—which both her mother and sister had ordered without the bun. They were crazy. Julie's Sweet Shoppe supplied the bakery goods for Magic Cafe and they were excellent. No way she was passing up this bun.

The meal dragged on forever, then Delbert and her father argued good-naturedly over who was going to pay the bill. They eventually agreed to split it. Delbert finally stood. "I'm sorry to break this up, but I really must get back to work. I need to go over to Sarasota and check on a few things at the hotel."

Camille gracefully swooped up from her seat. "I really do need to get to Mama's and help with the arrangements for the party. It's Friday night and I do hope I'll see you there."

Though Charlotte noticed Camille was looking directly at Eva when she said that comment.

Her father stood. "We should be going, too. I've got a tee time coming up with some old golfing buddies. Couldn't let a trip back to the island go by without a round of golf or two."

Thank goodness. It was over. She jumped up, too. "I better run."

"What's your hurry? You'll join us by the pool this afternoon, won't you?" Her mother asked.

It figured. Her mother and sister come all the way to Florida and stayed right on the beach… and they spend the day at the pool.

"I'm afraid I'm busy this afternoon."

"Fine. We'll see you tomorrow, then." Eva stood and grabbed her ever-so-coordinated-with-her-outfit purse.

Guess she was off the dinner list tonight. Which was fine by her.

"Oh, and Ben called. We're doing the boat trip tomorrow. Meet us at the marina at ten in the morning." Eva commanded. "And don't be late. We're not going to wait for you."

Okay, then.

She nodded and left the table while

everyone collected their things. She headed out the beach way while they all headed out to the parking lot for their cars. She slipped off her shoes as soon as she hit the sand and crossed down to the water's edge. She stood letting the waves wash over her feet and the wind lift her hair in the breeze.

Closing her eyes against the sun, she lifted her face to the bright warmth. She still needed to talk to her family, but it didn't look like tomorrow was going to be the day for it, either. No way she wanted to discuss all she wanted to say to them with Ben there.

But she would talk to them. She would.

She splashed her foot in the water with a kick at a wave. Relief rushed through her as she walked away from lunch, from her family, and from Eva and Camille and their constant chatter about nothing.

She now had a whole afternoon and evening of respite from all of that and she planned to paint until the light faded away.

CHAPTER 9

J ay sat on a barstool at Lucky Duck that evening. The assistant cook he'd hired was doing better, and he'd left early after the main dinner rush, leaving the assistant to finish up. He hoped he'd made the right decision...

Del Hamilton waved to him as he entered the tavern and slipped onto the stool beside him. Del motioned to Willie. "I'll have one of your special drinks, the one you call the basil motonic."

"Coming up."

"Thanks for meeting me. I needed a night away from Camille and her mother's constant planning for this party of theirs. You'd think it was the most important event of the year."

Jay grinned. "Probably is to Camille and

Mrs. Montgomery." He took a sip of his beer and grabbed some pretzels from the bowl on the bar. "Anyway, I was glad to take some time off myself. It's been busy at the inn. Lil is feeling better though and insisting she can take on more and more."

"So she's recovered from her fall?" Del reached for the drink Willie handed him and took a sip. "I swear, Willie, you come up with the best drinks anywhere."

Willie grinned. "Just wait until you taste this next one I'm working on."

"Let me know when you've perfected it."

"Will do." Willie left to wait on some new customers.

Jay took another sip of his beer then turned to Del. "I thought the Montgomerys were renting their beach house out now?"

Del sighed. "They are... but I rented it from them for the month so they could throw this party. They aren't quite used to not having the house any time they want to come down from Comfort Crossing and stay here at the beach house."

Jay stayed silent, sipping his beer, knowing Del would continue when he was ready. He'd learned that about the man. He liked to process his thoughts and choose his words carefully.

It was a strange friendship they had. Del was rich—*really rich*—and came from a powerful family that owned a whole string of hotels. And Jay was just a cook at an inn on the island. But they'd met when Del had stayed at the inn for a week and they hit it off. Now they often met for drinks when Del was in town. Though he was vividly aware of the fact that Camille didn't approve of him as a friend of Del's.

Del spun the straw, swirling his drink a few times. "I know everyone believes the Montgomerys are renting the house out because they don't want to come here as often." He sighed. "Not to be talking out of place, but that's not really the truth. They need to be scaling back on expenses. I probably shouldn't have rented the place for them. I mean, the Montgomerys are going to have to learn to cut corners. Camille is having a hard time with that, and so is her mother. But I refuse to keep bailing Camille out. I swear that woman can go through more money in a day than I go through in a year." He grinned and shrugged. "But, what can I say? She's my weakness. I do adore her—quirks and all."

Jay never could see what Del saw in Camille, but he kept his thoughts to himself.

Del took a sip of his drink and smiled. "So, Lil Charm would kill me, but my offer still stands to hire you out as a chef at the new hotel on Moonbeam Bay. Good pay, good benefits, and probably better hours than what you work now."

"Thanks, but I'm pretty content where I am. I love my job at the inn."

"And enjoying your job is an important part of a good life." Del nodded and raised his glass. "To enjoying life."

He clinked his glass with Del's. It was a great offer, but he was content with life here on Belle Island. He had enough money for all that he wanted. While it did appeal to him to try his hand at fancier fare, he couldn't imagine ever leaving Lil and the inn.

Charlotte sat out on the deck at The Nest with Robin and Sara. She propped her feet up on an ottoman, relaxing back in her chair. She really enjoyed the fact that now that the three of them were back on the island, they could get together like this again. She'd missed relaxing and chatting with them.

"How's the painting going?" Sara asked.

"Pretty good. I've almost finished the one I'm working on."

Robin grinned. "She painted when she was hiding out from her family this afternoon."

"I wasn't hiding. Not exactly. They were at the pool this afternoon and then... well, they didn't say what they were doing for dinner."

"Really?" Sara's eyes widened.

"Hey, I evidently wore the wrong clothes to lunch, *and* I ordered a beer."

Robin laughed. "Just trying to goad your mom?"

"I had to rush to order a beer before she ordered me another stupid Chardonnay."

"You hate Chardonnay." Sara frowned.

"Exactly. You know that. Robin knows that. Lil knows that. But my mother doesn't no matter how many times I tell her."

"Well, two days of them in town is over," Robin said helpfully.

"Tomorrow we're going out to Blue Heron Island with Ben."

"That should be fun. A trip there is always a

good time." Sara took a sip of her wine. "Right?"

"Depends on how big a boat Ben has…"

Robin laughed again. "Maybe he'll bring that trawler he has. He'd been working on fixing it up. It's pretty nice now. You could go up top. You know Eva would stay down below in the cabin."

"I can only hope."

"Hey, did you drop the rent checks at the office?" Robin leaned forward, changing the subject.

"I did." And she could do one more plus half the utilities. And food if she was lucky.

Robin frowned. "What's that look?"

"What look?" She did her best imitation of an innocent expression.

"That look you had when I asked you about the rent."

She let out a long sigh and turned to her friends. "I'm… I'm having a few money problems, is all."

"Not to be nosey… but didn't you make scads from your art in L.A.?" Sara asked.

How to answer that? "It wasn't scads, exactly. And it's expensive to live in L.A." She paused,

carefully choosing her words. "And I wasn't...
careful... with my funds."

"Didn't your agent—what was his name—
Reginald? Didn't he handle all that?"

She set her glass on the table. As long as they
knew she was broke, they might as well hear the
rest of it. "He did. I let him handle all of it. I
was silly and naive. We were actually a couple."

"You dated Reginald?"

"For a bit."

"What happened?"

"My art started not selling, and he started
not being interested in me anymore. Not as a
couple, not as an artist he represented."

"And the money?" Robin tilted her head to
the side.

"I heard he's in Europe these days. And I
assume he's there with what's left of
my money..."

"He stole from you?" Sara sat up straight.

"He came up with invoices and charges for
this and that and reasons why most of the
money was gone. But later I heard that he'd
done the same thing to another artist or two. He
was a charming scammer. I fell for it." She still
couldn't believe she'd been so gullible. The show

openings and being invited to fancy events in L.A. had gone to her head. Plus, Reginald was a good-looking guy and always managed to get invitations to every party. The more parties they went to, the more people they met who were interested in buying her work.

"That's terrible." Sara's eyes shone with sympathy.

"I was… foolish. It was all good until things started to slide downhill. I got up one morning and checked my social media accounts and there was Reginald with some new up-and-coming—and gorgeous—artist on his arm. I was no longer invited to the events with him. And I found out most of the money was gone."

"Take him to court." Robin frowned.

"I don't think he's planning on coming back stateside for quite some time. He's over hitting the art scene in Europe. With that same gorgeous artist on his arm."

"That's not right." Sara reached over and squeezed her hand.

"It's not, but it's what I let happen. I should never have given him that control."

"Then you will absolutely let Aunt Lil pay you for all the work you did on the cottages."

"I was just helping out."

Robin set her glass down. "Sara is right. There is no question. You're going to take money for the cottages. It was in the budget. And Lil wants to remodel two more rooms at the inn. We'll hire you for those, too."

"But—"

"Don't argue with Robin. You won't win." Sara grinned.

She looked from Robin to Sara... uncertain.

"I don't want charity."

"We either pay you, or we pay someone else. So we'll pay you." Robin shrugged—and her shrug was nothing like the dismissive shrug of her mother's. "And I still say you should show your new work to Paul Clark for his gallery."

"Robin... I told you I'm not ready for any showings."

"Okay, okay. But I'm going to keep bugging you about it."

"I know." She sighed. "I'd expect nothing less."

"And I'll win that argument soon, too." Robin scooped up her glass of wine, her look saying that she was confident of her future victory.

CHAPTER 10

Charlotte got up early the next day and sat in the kitchen, sipping coffee, gathering up her energy for a day with her family. Robin came into the kitchen, yawning, and reached for a mug.

"Morning. You're up early." Robin slipped into the chair across from her.

"Couldn't sleep."

"If you don't watch out, the island and I might turn you into a morning person."

A small smile tugged at the corners of her mouth. "I doubt it. But I do seem to be getting up a bit earlier these days."

"You got up earlier than *I* did. *That's* early."

"I was going to paint for a bit. Catch the morning light. But... I'm afraid I'll get all wrapped up in it and be late. I've been ordered by Eva to be on time."

"She's a bossy one." Robin sipped her coffee.

"She's—oh, never mind. She's my sister. She's never going to change." She tapped her fingers on the table. "I am going to talk to them this trip, though. Enough of this telling me to get a real job—though I might have to—and criticizing everything about my life."

"You go, girl."

"I'm an adult and it's time they treated me like one. I'm never going to fit into the mold they want. And I don't care. I don't want to be the person they want me to be."

"Man, I'd love to be around for this conversation." Robin grinned. "You going to talk to them today?"

"No, not with Ben around. I'll talk to them tomorrow. Sometime when we're alone."

"That's probably smart. You don't need an audience." She took a sip of her coffee. "Mmm. That's good." She took another sip.

"But I do need to figure out a way to earn a living. Especially while I don't have paintings that are selling."

"You know, you're great at painting and

fixing up old furniture. You could do that and sell it at Bella's on Oak Street. Bella is Josephine Clark's niece. Josephine is Paul Clark's wife. Anyway, Bella has a shop in Comfort Crossing, Mississippi, but recently opened a shop here on the island, too. Vintage items, beach decor, and things like that. There are always people looking to find cute pieces when they buy new places here on the island. It could help tide you over until you sell more of your paintings."

She chewed her lip. She did enjoy fixing up the furniture and painting it. She'd found a discarded dresser someone was throwing out, fixed it up, and painted it in shades of teal and mint green, then painted seashells on the front of it for her bedroom.

"I'll get Bella's phone number for you and you can talk to her." Robin's face was covered in a self-satisfied smile.

"For once, I'm not going to argue with you. I think that would be a great idea. I'll talk to Bella and see if she's interested and what she thinks might sell in her shop."

"Perfect." Robin stood. "I better go get ready. Why don't you go paint for a bit and set a timer so you're not late to meet up with your family?"

Charlotte stood and took her mug over to the sink. "That's a good idea. I'm not up for another lecture on punctuality. I'm actually pretty much always on time... except when meeting up with my family."

Ben got up early to get the boat ready for their trip to Blue Heron Island. He'd only taken Lady Belle out for a couple of short trips since he'd overhauled the engine. The boat had been his father's pride and joy. An older boat, to be sure, but she was a beaut.

He'd refinished the weathered teak and replaced a few pieces. Put new flooring in the main cabin and recovered the seats in there. The galley had been updated. He'd also put a nice new mattress in the cabin below deck. He had plans to move out of the place he was renting at Bayside Bungalows and live on the trawler once all the renovations were finished. He had the end slip at one of the docks at the marina with a fabulous view of the bay. Perks of being the owner.

He balanced the bags with box lunches he'd picked up from Jay at the inn and climbed aboard. They carried ice, soda, and bottled water at the marina shop. He'd better go grab some of those.

As he climbed back off the boat, he saw Charlotte heading down the dock toward him, her arms full. He hurried to help her. "What's all this?"

"I stopped by The Sweet Shoppe and got some cookies, and then I made this container of sweet tea. I didn't know what all you'd have and what we'd need."

"This is great. Let me put it aboard, then I'm headed to get bottled water and soda and ice from the shop."

Charlotte eyed the boat with appreciation. "Wow, look at this. Your dad's old boat. She looks beautiful."

His chest swelled with pride at her compliment. "Thank you. I've been working on it off and on for a few years. I'm going to live on her when I'm finished."

"On a boat?" She looked out at the bay. "With that view? That sounds like heaven to me."

"I think so, too."

He helped her climb aboard and she followed him to the galley. "Ben, this is wonderful. It's like a tiny house… only a boat." Her laugh rang through the boat. "I love it."

"Here, I'll show you around." He proudly showed her how he'd upped the kitchen space by redoing the cabinets to a more efficient arrangement. He'd enlarged the bathroom slightly by taking out a closet but added more storage under the seating in the main cabin. He'd found new places to tuck items and increase the storage while still making sure there was plenty of room to walk around and the boat didn't feel cramped.

"This is wonderful. It's so pretty. I just love it." Charlotte finished the tour. "I can't wait to take it out to the island."

"Let's go grab those drinks, then we're ready as soon as your family gets here. I've got some beach chairs and an umbrella stored so we can go to the beach on the island if anyone wants to."

"I love going shelling there."

He grinned. "Then good thing I put in a couple of buckets, too."

They climbed off the boat and went to the shop at the marina. He loaded up on drinks and dumped them in a rolling cart that he toted back to the boat. After hauling the drinks aboard and stashing them in the fridge, they settled on the seats out on the stern, waiting for the Duncans to arrive.

"I know I'm early. I was late yesterday meeting them for lunch at Magic Cafe. Didn't want to make that mistake again." Charlotte flipped her hair back away from her face and dug a hat out of her tote bag. "I try and keep the sun off my face." She placed the hat on her head, and he thought she looked like someone out of a beach life magazine. A healthy glow, and long tanned legs. She wore simple denim shorts and a chambray shirt tied at her waist. The bright red flip-flops completed her outfit. He noticed a few specks of teal and yellow paint on the back of her hands. Hazard of her career, he imagined.

"Oh, there they are." Charlotte, oblivious that he'd been staring at her—thank goodness for his sunglasses—waved to her family. Her smile was a bit forced, though. He could tell that much.

He turned and hopped off the boat to help them aboard.

CHAPTER 11

C harlotte smiled and waved to her family, determined to have a fabulous day on this fabulous boat. Everything was going to be... *fabulous.*

Ben helped Eva and her mother aboard. Eva looked around the area on the back of the boat. "Oh, do we have to sit out in the sun?"

"No, come on into the cabin. It has air conditioning."

"Oh, good. This Florida heat and humidity is killing me."

Though, to be honest, Charlotte thought that Eva looked picture-perfect, as always.

"So, you're on time today." Eva looked at her.

"She was helping me get things all set up." Ben defended her.

Though she didn't need defending, not really. But it was nice to feel like at least one person on this trip didn't think she was a total loser. She pasted on a smile. "Didn't want to keep you waiting."

Her mother and sister went into the cabin, closing the door behind them to keep in the cool air. Right then she decided she'd just relax out here on the seats at the back and enjoy the fresh air.

"Give me a tour of the boat, son. It looks good. I hear you've been working on it." Her father and Ben disappeared inside.

She propped her feet up on the cushion of the seat beside her. Yes, this was a nice place to sit for the trip.

After giving her father a tour, Ben cast off the lines, and they headed out into the bay. The sea breeze picked up as they left the bay and headed out into open water. Before long, her father went in to join her mom and sister.

Ben motioned to her to join him up top on the upper steering thingy—whatever it was called up there. She climbed the ladder and stood beside him, one hand holding onto her hat in the strong breeze. She finally gave up on it and stashed it in a cubby Ben pointed to.

"This is… fabulous. I love it up here. It's like we're on top of the world."

"I like navigating from up here instead of down in the cabin when I can."

"My mom and sister found the bottle of Chardonnay you had chilling, so I'm pretty sure they're set for a bit. Dad poured a scotch."

"Did you bring your suit? You want to go for a swim on the island?"

"I have it on under my shorts. I'd love to go for a swim. I'm not sure that's in the plans though. Eva doesn't really swim in the ocean." She frowned. She didn't think her sister even liked to walk on the beach. Choosing this outing to Blue Heron Island seemed like a strange choice.

"Well, I love swimming in the gulf."

A pair of pelicans sat on the channel markers as they passed by. Seagulls flew overhead, and she looked where Ben pointed and saw dolphins frolicking beside the boat.

"This is amazing. We never had a boat when we lived here. I only occasionally went out on one growing up when I'd get invited. I can't believe you can just go out here like this whenever you want."

"Pretty much. Well, as long as I can afford the gas." He grinned and his eyes sparkled.

Blue Heron Island came into view. She turned at the sound of someone coming up the ladder. It was Eva.

"I see we're almost there." She came and stood right next to Ben, flashing him that smile of hers. The one that made grown men fall to their knees. "Do you think I could steer the boat?"

"Uh... I guess."

Eva slipped in front of Ben and put her hands on the steering wheel. She leaned back against Ben and laughed. "This is fun. I'm captain of the ship."

She noticed that Ben didn't let go of the wheel while Eva played captain. He let her steer for a bit, his hands resting near hers.

She turned and looked out across the water, ignoring Eva, and a bit ticked off her sister had ruined the perfectly good time she was having with Ben. But then, that's what Eva did best. Walk into a room and claim the undivided attention of every male.

"I think I'll go back down." Charlotte

climbed down the ladder and went back to where she'd been sitting before.

Soon Ben—she was sure it was Ben, not Eva —deftly steered Lady Belle to the docks on one side of the island. Her father helped him tie up.

"We're all set now. Time for that beach picnic." Ben started gathering supplies.

"It's so hot," Eva complained.

"Of course we'll picnic on the beach," her father countered.

"I have a pop-up shelter. It should help keep off most of the sun," Ben offered.

"Perfect. Let's get this picnic started." Her father filled his arms with chairs and the umbrella.

Ben got a beach cart out and loaded it with food and drinks and the pop-up shelter. They all trudged over to the sea side of the island and Ben set up the shelter. Her mother and sister grabbed chairs and sat under the shade of the pop-up. Ben spread out a blanket on the sand in front of the shelter. Charlotte helped him unpack the lunches and drinks.

The sea breeze kept the area pleasantly cool even though Eva complained about the heat and the sand.

As soon as she finished eating, she grabbed a

plastic pail, wanting to escape Eva's complaints. "I'm going to go shelling."

"In this heat? Can't we go back to the boat and the air-conditioning?" Eva fanned herself with a napkin.

"I'll go shelling with you." Ben jumped up and turned to her family. "We'll be back soon. Then we'll head back to Belle Island."

"Take your time, son. I think I'll grab another one of those sandwiches and maybe a beer." Her father rummaged through the food, then sat down with his sandwich and beer.

Charlotte headed to the edge of the water and bent down and picked up a perfect shell. Well, it seemed perfect to her. A pink-lilac color lined its gentle curves. Ben fell into step beside her and they rounded the bend of the island, no longer in sight of her family. Once they were out of sight, she sucked in a deep breath of the fresh, salty air. This island felt like paradise to her. Sunshine. Waves. And they hadn't seen one other person so far.

"Wanna go swimming?" Ben eyed her.

"I do." She set down her bucket and peeled off her shorts and shirt. "Last one in is a rotten egg."

Been whooped and rushed past her,

dropping his shirt on the sand as he sped toward the water. With a leap, he jumped the waves and dove underwater. She laughed and splashed through the water, trying to catch up with him.

He erupted from the waves beside her and scooped her up, grabbing her around the waist and spinning around. She laughed out loud. A laugh that came from somewhere deep inside of her. Just pure joy. Enjoying the water, enjoying the sun. Enjoying… Ben.

They splashed and ducked and laughed like two little kids in the surf. When they finally tired, they sat on a rock near the beach to dry off.

"That was the most fun I've had in… well, I don't know when I've had that much fun." She stretched out her legs, balancing on the rock.

The sun shone on a few streaks of golden hair woven through Ben's brown locks. His face was tanned with a bit of pink from the sun and breeze from today. He shook his head and droplets of water flew everywhere. She laughed again.

"Nothing like a quick dip in the sea." He grinned at her.

"There isn't. A pool is just—"

"It pales in comparison, doesn't it?"

"It does." She nodded, then sighed. She glanced up at the sky and saw some clouds approaching. Typical Florida afternoon. "I guess we should head back. I'm sure my sister is more than ready to get back to the air conditioning."

He jumped up and reached out. She took his strong hand, and he pulled her off the rock. With a quick swoop, he grabbed her pail of shells and scooped up their clothes. She jumped on one foot slipping her shorts back on and pulled the shirt over her suit. He pulled on his shirt, covering his strong, tanned shoulders. Too bad. Not that she'd been staring at his hard abs *or* his broad shoulders…

They headed back to the shelter.

When they got back, Eva was pacing back and forth under the small canopy. "Where have you been? There's a storm coming in." She pointed to clouds gathering in the distance.

Ben looked at them and frowned. "Looks like we might get a small squall. They weren't predicting much chance of them today but looks like they were wrong."

Her father and Ben took down the canopy and gathered up all their belongings, and then they all headed back toward the dock. Halfway there, the heavens opened and rain began to pelt them.

Eva screamed like a little girl, held a towel above her, and raced for the boat. Her mother followed close behind.

"I've got these things. You get the ladies on board." Ben nodded to her father who hurried after Eva and her mother. He turned to her. "You can go ahead, too."

"I'm already wet from swimming. The rain won't hurt me." They tugged on the cart and made their way back to the dock. Ben made quick work of loading all their things back on the boat, then reached a hand to help her board.

They went into the cabin where Eva was curled up in a blanket. Her mother sat with another blanket thrown around her shoulders and didn't look pleased. At all. They both looked at Ben like the weather was his fault.

"I'll get us back to the marina. It might be kind of a rough ride, though."

"Are you sure the boat will be okay in this storm?" Eva frowned.

"She will. She's a sturdy one."

"I'll go untie her." Charlotte offered. Ben nodded.

KAY CORRELL

She untied the bow, then the stern, and her father helped her back on board. Ben steered them away from the dock, and they headed back out to sea.

The boat rocked and bobbed on the waves. Eva turned positively green. "This is the worst day ever," she moaned.

Charlotte didn't agree. It had been a… *fabulous* day.

The storm blew over as quickly as it had come up. By the time they reached the marina, the sun broke through the clouds. She turned to Ben and smiled. "Such is Florida weather."

"I'm sorry we got caught in that storm though. It was a rough ride back. I don't think Eva feels very good." He expertly docked the boat and one of the marina workers tied them up.

Ben hurried to help her family disembark. "I'm sorry about the rough weather, Eva."

"She'll be fine. Just needs to get on solid ground for a bit," her father answered. "I'll get the women back to the inn and they can have a little rest." He looked up at the sky. "I think I might still be able to get in nine holes of golf this afternoon."

Charlotte watched her family head down the

dock. Without saying a word of goodbye to her. Nor did she hear Eva thank Ben for taking them out on the boat, even though it had been her idea.

Ben climbed back onboard. "I don't think that day went exactly as Eva had planned."

Charlotte laughed. "Not quite."

Ben looked up, shielding his eyes from the sun. "Now that the weather is nice again, do you want to join me for a drink?"

"Sure, where?"

"I was thinking right here on the boat…"

"That sounds perfect."

"How about some of your sweet tea?"

"Yes, that sounds nice."

"I'll grab some towels and finish drying off the seats and we can sit back here and watch the world go by."

"Can't think of anything I'd rather do."

Ben headed into the cabin, thinking about the day. He didn't know what had changed over the years. Eva was so different, or maybe he'd changed, but the Eva on this boat trip was not like the Eva in his memories. Though, he had to admit, even soaked from the rain, she still looked beautiful. He didn't know how some women did that.

He poured the tea and grabbed a couple of towels. Now Charlotte, she looked... soaked. And adorable. Her face had pinked up, and her coppery locks of hair danced in the wind, drying from the swim and the rainstorm. And she seemed unfazed by all of it. Which he also found adorable.

He walked back to the stern, handed her a glass, then quickly dried off the seats. They sat facing the bay, with their feet propped up on a cooler.

He watched while she took her first sip of the icy tea.

"Oh, that's good." She wiped her mouth and grinned at him.

"Nothing better than a cold glass of sweet tea on a sunny afternoon." He took a sip of his.

They watched a few boats head past them out on the bay. A center-console boat laden with fishing rods. A tri-toon with a group of laughing teens. A sailboat came into the bay under motor.

He sighed. He loved everything about the marina and the bay and the gulf. He couldn't wait to finish up the renovations and move aboard the Lady Belle.

"This is just wonderful," Charlotte said after a while. "I could sit here for hours and just watch the boats and the clouds."

He pointed over between the docks. "Looks like the manatees have come to play, too."

Charlotte stood and looked where he was pointing. "I love watching them. They are so big and, I don't know—so homely they're beautiful?"

He laughed. "Haven't heard them described that way, but I'll give you that."

She sat back down beside him, her fingers grazing his as she settled on the seat.

The thought shot through him that he wanted to entwine his fingers with hers, and he stared down at their hands, side by side on the seat.

Where had *that* thought come from?

They'd been friends in high school. Not even close friends, they just ran with the same group.

And now he wanted to hold her hand?

She lifted her other hand to shield the sun from her eyes and looked out at the water. Then she took her hand that was next to his and reached for her glass.

And just like that, the moment was gone.

She turned to face him then, her face serious. "So, you know what you said to me the other day? About I'm the only one who needs to be proud of myself?"

He nodded.

"I've decided to have a talk with my family. They don't really count my artistic endeavors as work and discount everything I do in that field. But it's time I quit listening to all that. I love painting. And Robin came up with the idea that I could paint some furniture for sale in a shop on Oak Street to help bring in some more cash."

That surprised him. He'd seen articles regarding her work, and he thought she'd probably made some pretty decent money off of sales of her paintings. He wondered why she needed the cash, but it wasn't really a question he could ask.

"I remodeled some cottages for Lil and redid some furnishing. I really enjoyed it. I can buy some old tables, dressers, and chairs and paint them. I did one for our cottage. A dresser for my room and painted some seashells on it. If they want things like that for sale at the shop, maybe I could sell there on commission."

"Bella's store?"

She nodded. "I'm sure my family will still not think it's a fitting way to earn money. It's not a job like Eva's—I heard she's up for some big promotion—but creating things is what I like to do. It's what makes me happy."

"Being happy in your work is important. I love working here at the marina. Love everything about it. Sometimes I get tired of going to boat shows and traveling to the other marinas and things like that. I'd much rather be here tinkering with a boat."

"Does your brother work here too? He was younger than us by quite a bit, right?"

"No, he lives in Michigan. He didn't want anything to do with the marina and couldn't wait to leave the island." Ben laughed. "Yet, he lives a five-minute walk from Lake Michigan, in a small town up there."

A phone chimed, and he waited while Charlotte dug it out of her tote. She checked the message and frowned. "Eva texted. She said that Camille needs to know if we're all coming to her mother's party on Friday. I was thinking of begging off, but that seems cowardly. I used to go to big parties all the time in L.A. to get my name known. There's no reason I can't do that here, too. These are people that live in the big houses on the island or mainland. They're from all around here and Mississippi. Wouldn't hurt to meet them."

"That's the spirit."

"Eva said Camille said we could each bring a plus one. But then she texted that of course *I* wouldn't have one..." She turned and looked directly at him. "Would you... I mean... it wouldn't really be a date or anything, but would you be a plus one? Would you go with me?"

"Sure." He nodded. "I'm not much on fancy parties, but, yes, I'll go with you. I'll probably feel all out of place among the fancy people."

Charlotte laughed. "And I'm sure my sister will let me know that I've dressed inappropriately and tell me anything and everything I'm doing wrong."

"Sounds fun." He gave her an exaggerated grin, then rolled his eyes.

"I'll text her back and say I'm coming with a date. Well, not a date-date." She looked up quickly from her phone.

He smiled and nodded. Though, to be honest, he wouldn't mind calling it a date...

When she finished the text, she reached out and touched his hand. An electric shock spiked through him and he swallowed. Then swallowed again.

"Thanks, Ben. I appreciate it. Always helps to have a friend at your side at stuff like this."

She took her hand away, and he brought his now lonely hand up to rub his chin.

A friend. She thought of him as a friend.

CHAPTER 12

R obin walked into Paul Clark's gallery and looked around at the art on display. There were paintings and photographs and a section of carved wooden sea captains. She smiled and walked over to a foot-high carving of a sea captain with a long yellow slicker and rain boots. He looked just like she imagined the old man who used to run the lighthouse might have looked on a stormy day.

"Robin, how great to see you." Paul walked up to her. "What brings you into the gallery?"

"I was wondering if you could give me Bella's phone number. I have a friend—Charlotte Duncan—do you remember her? Anyway, she's moved back here to the island and we're rooming together at Bayside Bungalows. She's an artist, and she's trying to earn a bit more cash. She did some wonderful work for Lil at the inn, painting furniture. Very coastal looking. I thought I could connect her with Bella and maybe she could do some furniture on consignment for her shop."

"Bella's up in Comfort Crossing right now at her main shop, but I've got one of her cards right over here."

She followed Paul to a small table in the back corner. He handed her Bella's card. "She's always looking for unique items to sell in the shop."

"Thanks."

"You said your friend was an artist."

"She's a very talented painter."

Paul's eyes brightened. "I'm doing a showing of local artists. Do you think she'd be interested? I just had a cancellation. The artist can't get the work to me in time. So now I have some wall space left to fill. I really need to get things wrapped up in the next few days, though. What kind of paintings does Charlotte do?"

"Right now she's working on a series of paintings of the beach and town. They're fabulous. When you look at them, it's like you can imagine yourself right in the scene. They are so… I can't describe them in proper artistic terms, but they are emotional and… well, I think they're fabulous."

"That sounds perfect and would fit in well with this exhibit. Do you think I could see her work?"

"We could head to the bungalow and see it now." Had she really just suggested that? But what was that saying? A bird in the hand, etcetera? Or was this more strike while the iron was hot? Anyway…when Charlotte found out she might kill her… But she was going to do it anyway. Char just needed a little nudge to get back in the game.

"I do have time now. Would you care to walk? I could use the fresh air."

They headed over to the bungalow, leisurely walking down the sidewalks, in and out of the sunshine. They chatted about the weather and Lil's recovery and the new butter crumb muffin Julie was offering at The Sweet Shoppe. Typical small-town chatter. She smiled as they ambled along. She loved the easy pace here on the island and even loved how everyone knew everyone else's business.

Well, *usually* loved it. Sometimes it was hard

to get much privacy, but she'd gotten used to it over the years.

They got to the bungalow, and she opened the door. "Charlotte? You here?" She wasn't sure if she wanted Charlotte to be here or to be gone. Anyway, silence greeted her so that answered that question.

"Come in." She led Paul to the brightly lit room Charlotte was using as her studio. She flipped around some of the paintings and leaned them against the walls around the room, all the while hoping she was doing the right thing. Charlotte was just too critical of her new work and didn't think she was ready to show it. That agent had done a number on her confidence, and her parents being in town wasn't helping things.

Maybe if Paul liked it, Charlotte would begin to believe in her work again.

Paul walked around the room, looking at them with a critical eye. His face broke into a wide smile. "These *are* fabulous. You were right. Do you think she'd pick a handful and we could hang them in the exhibit? I could talk to her about pricing them, or maybe she already has a figure in mind. I usually get quite a few sales from these local shows."

Robin took a deep breath. "I'm sure she'll be pleased." Maybe. After she got around to explaining to Charlotte how she'd shown her paintings to Paul behind her back…

"Perfect. Here's my card." He took a card out of his wallet. "Could you have her call me this evening or tomorrow morning and let me know?"

She reached out and took the card. "I'll have her call."

Or she'd be calling and explaining how Charlotte was never speaking to her again and didn't want a thing to do with the show…

CHAPTER 13

Charlotte looked out at the bay, loathe to head back to her bungalow. A day in the fresh air and sunshine—well, mostly sunshine—had done her good. She'd never have thought she'd be able to relax like this with her family just a short walk away.

"I've got leftover snacks. We could do some cheese and crackers and I'll see what else I can rustle up. You've stayed this long. Might as well stay for the sunset." Ben leaned forward, ready to stand.

"I'd like that."

"I've got a bottle of red wine we could crack open."

"Sounds lovely."

Ben headed inside and she should probably

follow him in and help get things ready, but she was feeling very relaxed and lazy, sitting here in the fading sunshine. She stretched like a cat and leaned back on the cushions.

He returned soon with a tray of food and wine. He popped up a table from what seemed like nowhere and placed the tray on it.

She grinned. "More hidden storage."

"I seriously looked at a million pictures and videos of boats when I started rehabbing Lady Belle. I scoured the internet for clever storage ideas."

"I'd say you did a great job."

He sent her a grateful smile. "Thanks."

She watched the sun shine on his face as he concentrated on his tasks, then plopped down next to her on the seat. He poured two glasses of wine and handed one to her. "To a picture-perfect sunset."

"To the sunset." She raised her glass and touched it lightly to his.

His long, tanned fingers wrapped around his glass as he brought it up to his lips and took a sip. She realized she was staring at him and ducked her head. She took a sip of the wine and looked out at the bay.

Not at Ben.

Soon, she couldn't help herself and stole another look in his direction. He was staring out at the bay, lost in thought. But it seemed like he could feel her staring at him, and he slowly turned to look at her and a small smile tipped up the corners of his mouth.

Ben Hallet had morphed from a gawky teen into a handsome man. Not that it mattered, because he was one of the masses that flocked around Eva, doing her bidding, falling for her charms.

So there was no need to even think about Ben as handsome. Or interesting. Or... well, as anything but an acquaintance, a friend.

She gave him a small smile in return and turned to watch the sunset. It did not disappoint, with a glorious display of oranges fading into dark blue.

"Belle Island is known for those sunsets." Ben's quiet voice broke their silence.

"It is just... beautiful." She spoke in hushed tones, not wanting to break the magic.

Ben stirred beside her and stood with a long sigh. "I should get this cleared up and we should probably head back to the bungalows."

"Here, let me help." She stood.

He shook his head. "Nah, I got it. Enjoy the

113

last few minutes of the sunset. It will only take a few minutes for me to get this all put away." He disappeared into the cabin.

Suddenly she was sitting there all by herself and felt alone, which was strange because she usually liked being alone and was comfortable with it. She stared at the doorway to the cabin.

Why now? Why was she feeling lonely *now*?

She felt... she felt like she just didn't quite belong anywhere. She didn't truly fit in back here in Belle Island yet. The locals eyed her as a bit of a traitor for moving away. Or maybe she imagined that. She sure didn't fit in with her family—she never had.

And now she was having crazy thoughts about Ben. A man who she'd always thought was smitten with her sister. Not that he would ever look at her as anything more than a friend, especially not with Eva batting her eyelashes at him.

She turned and looked up at the stars that were beginning to appear in the endless sky stretching above her. How had she let herself become this person? And more importantly, what was she going to do to change things?

Charlotte walked back to the bungalows with Ben. They didn't talk much, just slowly made their way back home. It was a comfortable silence, though. She did feel comfortable just being with Ben.

Still, she reminded herself that was a problem. He was just a friend. And he probably would have preferred if Eva had asked him to Camille's party. He'd probably hang around Eva at the party anyway. Most men did.

They got to the door and she turned to him. "Thanks for taking us out on your boat, and thanks for the nice evening and watching the sunset."

"I had a good day," he said simply. Then he turned and headed across the courtyard to his own bungalow.

She turned the handle and stepped inside. Robin was sitting on the couch, leafing through a magazine. "Oh, good. You're home."

"I am." She sank onto a chair across from Robin.

"How was the boat trip to Blue Heron Island?"

"It was… fun. We got hit by a storm though and Eva wasn't very happy. But by the time we got back, the sun was shining again. Then I stayed for a bit on Ben's boat."

Robin sat forward. "And?"

"And, nothing. You know he has a crush on Eva. We just talked, then had some left-over food and some wine. Watched the sunset."

"And?"

"And nothing. Again. He's one of those men who Eva wraps around her finger, and I'm just not interested in competing with that."

"If you say so. I'm just saying Ben is a great guy."

"Can we drop it?" She sighed.

Robin stood and paced the floor. "Since you're already annoyed with me…"

She cocked her head and waited for Robin to continue.

"I did something that maybe you're going to be a tiny bit mad at me about."

"I don't get mad at you." She shook her head.

"Good, then I'll tell you what I did. I showed your work to Paul Clark and he wants to add some of your paintings to a local artist exhibit he's having at the gallery." Robin rushed out the words.

"You what?" She jumped up from her chair. "You didn't."

"I did." Robin nodded. "And, for the record, he loved your new work. Said it would fit in great with the exhibit."

Anger rushed through her. How could Robin have done this? "But I'm not ready. I *said* I wasn't ready. This wasn't *your* choice to make."

"I just thought you needed a little push. Don't be mad," Robin begged.

"I *am* mad. This should have been my decision. *Mine.*" Her anger boiled over. "I am sick and tired of people always thinking they know what is best for me. What I should be doing. Making decisions for me. *Sick* of it." She stomped her foot.

Robin sank onto the couch. "I'm sorry, Char. I didn't look at it that way. I was just trying to help, not trying to run your life."

"And yet, you did this without asking." She turned and headed back to her room.

"I really am sorry," Robin called after her.

She ignored Robin, went into her bedroom, and closed the door firmly behind her. She kicked off her shoes and flopped onto the bed. Why did her life seem so out of control right now? It had been ever since Reginald had dumped her and she'd realized he'd pilfered so much of her money.

And why was she thinking of it as *pilfered*? That was too nice of a word for what he did. He *stole* her money.

And she let him. And she let her family walk all over her. And now Robin…

She closed her eyes and threw her arm across her face.

Things needed to change.

CHAPTER 14

The next morning Charlotte hid out in her studio with her morning coffee, avoiding Robin. She understood why Robin had shown her work to Paul and she understood Robin thought she was helping. But it was still her decision and she wasn't ready to show this new work. Not yet.

She turned at the sound of a light rap at the door.

"Can I come in?"

She sighed. So much for avoiding her roomie. "Yes."

Robin came in and handed her a blueberry muffin from The Sweet Shoppe. "Will bribery help you get over being mad at me?"

She took the offered bribe. "Maybe."

"I am sorry. I'll call Paul this morning and tell him you won't be putting your work in his show."

"I appreciate that." She took a bite of the muffin. "But, I'm still mad at you." A slight smile teased the corners of her mouth, full of the delightful treat— her favorite kind of muffin.

"But you'll forgive me?"

She took another bite. "Soon. I'll forgive you soon."

"There's another muffin on the counter in the kitchen." Robin grinned, then walked over to perch on a stool beside the window. Her face grew serious. "I know I messed up. I realize now that you're fighting all these people controlling your life. Especially with your family in town. I know they've never been... uh... supportive of you. I shouldn't have interfered."

"Thanks for understanding. I've got to figure all this out on my own."

"And I need to give you the space to do that."

"Thanks, Robin." Charlotte smiled at Robin, unable to remain mad at her friend for long, especially when she genuinely seemed sorry for interfering.

A knock came from their front door. Robin jumped up. "I'll get it."

Charlotte stood in front of her painting, eyeing it. It still needed something…

"Uh, Char?"

She turned to face the doorway.

"Paul Clark is here to see you. I told him you weren't interested in the show, but he wants to talk to you."

"Tell him I'm busy."

Paul stepped out from behind Robin.

She sucked in a deep breath. *Oops.* "Ah… Mr. Clark."

"Paul. Please, call me Paul." He entered the room. "I understand that Robin and I misstepped a bit. I didn't mean to cause any trouble. But I wanted you to know that your work is good. Really good. Emotional. And your use of color is excellent. If you don't want to exhibit in the local artists show, I'd be willing to give you a full showing of your own."

She sat down on the stool in front of her easel. "You… *what?*"

"A showing of your own. I'm sure your work

would be very popular. Is this something you'd be interested in?"

She sat and stared at him. A showing of her own? She hadn't had one in so long, and this work was so different from her previous work.

But hadn't she just promised herself last night that things were going to change?

She stood and crossed over to where Paul was standing near the doorway. "Yes, I'd be interested."

She didn't miss the grin on Robin's face.

"Great. We can meet and discuss what pieces you'd like to show." Do you have an agent I should contact?"

Robin stifled a laugh.

"Um… no agent at the moment."

"Would you also consider showing a few at the local artist exhibit? It would start to get your name out there before your private showing."

"I…" She paused, turned to look at Robin and rolled her eyes, then turned back to Paul. "Yes, that sounds good."

"How about we pick out a few pieces?"

She just nodded, a bit stunned from how quickly all this was moving.

"Oh, and Mrs. Montgomery usually showcases a few pieces of artwork at the parties she throws. She's having one tomorrow. I usually supply the artwork and set it up. I'd love to show that painting you did with the dog on the beach and the man tossing a piece of driftwood for him. That's Noah and Cooper in the painting, isn't it?"

"It is. You want to show it at Camille's party?"

"Yes, will that work for you?"

"You want to show my work at the Montgomerys' party?"

"Snap out of it, Char. He loves your work." Robin crossed over and draped a hand across her shoulders. "Your choice. Yes or no. You probably should say, yes, though. You know, if you want to." She grinned.

"Yes."

Paul broke into a wide smile. "Excellent. Now, let's choose some other paintings for the gallery and we'll get out of your hair and let you paint."

And just like that, she was back in the art world.

But would anyone want to *buy* this new style of her art?

Ben decided to drop by his mother's and check on her on his way to work. Maybe he could convince her to come to the marina with him today.

But he doubted she'd say yes...

"Mom? You home?" He walked in the back door to her house.

"Ben, did we have plans?"

"Can't a son drop in and visit his mom?"

"Of course, dear. I always love to see you, but I'm just leaving."

"Where are you headed?" He tried to sound nonchalant, but he hoped it was more than a trip to the grocery store.

"Dorothy invited me to the knitting group at the community center. I thought I might go over there and check it out. I'm in the middle of knitting a baby sweater and booties. Have no idea who it's for, but I like to have baby gifts on hand." She gathered up her knitting bag.

"I could walk over with you," he offered, glad to see she was actually going.

"You don't need to do that."

"It's a nice day and you know I love to walk."

"Okay, let me grab my purse and I'm ready."

"I can carry your knitting bag." He eyed the big floral bag and a brief thought crossed his mind on whether it would affect his manhood to carry that big, loud, very floral bag. He rolled his eyes at himself. He'd carry the darn thing if it meant his mother was getting out of the house and visiting with people.

She laughed. "No, I've got it. It's not heavy."

They headed to the community center, a short five-minute walk away. They entered the building and Ben waved to Noah standing down the hallway. They walked to the room where the knitters were meeting.

Dorothy saw them and jumped up and came over. "Ruby, I'm so glad you decided to join us. We've got coffee on, and Mary Lou brought some baked goods from The Sweet Shoppe. Come in, let me introduce you to anyone you don't know."

Another woman walked up. "Hi, I'm Mary."

"Glad to meet you."

His mother took a tentative step into the room, and he smiled and nodded at her.

"I'll see you later, son."

"Bye, Mom."

He turned to leave, feeling like he'd just

dropped a young child off at her first day of school. Not that he had kids. But... still.

Noah came down the hallway. "I see you convinced Ruby to come."

"Not me. It was all Dorothy's work. Hope Mom has a good time."

"I'm sure she will. A fine group of ladies."

"I'm just happy to get her out of the house. Get her interested in something."

"Maybe after she gets more comfortable coming here, she'll join another group." Noah's voice sounded hopeful.

"Hope so. Well, I should be heading to the marina. I just wanted to walk Mom over." He hoped it all would work out and his mom would get involved here at the community center. "Catch you later."

He turned and made his way out of the center and over to the marina. He had to finish up repairs on two boats that had gotten a bit delayed. He'd been busy prepping a huge yacht they'd sold for delivery. The sale of the yacht would be a welcome influx of cash for the marina. He kept a few slips on the docks for people to leave their boats they wanted to sell. He'd show the boats and play middleman. This time it had paid off quite well. The marina did well, but it seemed like something always needed fixing or repaired.

He hoped to have time to finish up a few things on Lady Belle too. He glanced at his watch. It was shaping up to be a busy day and he was already getting a late start.

CHAPTER 15

"I can't believe Eva sent over a dress for me to wear tonight." Charlotte glared at the box sitting on her bed. "She and Mom went shopping in Sarasota yesterday and evidently found this proper outfit for me." She yanked the box open and pulled out a fitted pale green sheath dress and matching flats to show Robin.

"It's pretty?" Robin asked it more as a question than a statement. Then she sighed. "But it sure doesn't look like you."

"I should probably wear it." She sighed.

"Try it on."

Charlotte slipped on the pale green dress and looked in the mirror. "Oh, heck no. I'm not wearing this. I look like some kind of dress-up doll stuffed into a fashion dress. I wouldn't even be able to breathe. And this pale color makes me look positively anemic."

"It's a pretty dress... in a stuffy kind of way." Robin got off the bed and walked over to stand beside her. "But it's so not you. Let's dig around in your closet and find something else."

Soon Robin had pulled out a flowing printed skirt and white blouse. "This will work."

She slipped on the outfit and Robin handed her a belt for a finishing touch.

"I... I think I like it?" She spun around looking at the outfit from all angles in the mirror.

"You've got those cute red flats you can wear with it."

"You think I'll look okay? I'll fit in at the party?"

"You look stunning. Very artist-like." Robin spun her around to look in the full-length mirror. "You want me to French braid your hair, or do you want to wear it down?"

"Down, I think." She sighed. "And I'm pretty sure my mom is not going to like this outfit."

"She's crazy then. You look great. Add a touch of lipstick and you're all set."

They both paused when they heard a knock

at the door. "That will be Ben. I'll get it." Robin disappeared from the room.

She put on the tiniest bit of lipstick and looked in the mirror again. She did look artsy if she did say so herself. She'd always worn free-spirited, bohemian outfits in L.A. Most of the people had come to expect it of her. She did not have to squeeze into the ridiculous dress her mother had sent over. She'd just thank her mother, nicely, and hope things didn't blow up in her face.

Ben let out a low whistle when Charlotte walked into the room. "Wow." He didn't really know what to add to that. She looked stunning. The outfit she had on suited her perfectly.

She smoothed her hands along her sides. "It's okay?"

"It's more than okay. You look... great. *Really* great."

She smiled at his compliment.

"Okay, you two kids run along to your fancy party." Robin opened the door.

"I wish you were coming." She grabbed

Robin's hand. "I could use all the reinforcements I can get tonight.

"You'll do fine." Robin hugged her. "Now, go. Meet the fancy people. Get your name out there."

He stood out on the porch with her, unable to take his eyes off this artsy, accomplished woman beside him. What was he doing taking an accomplished artist to a fancy party where he'd know no one? So out of his league. He cleared his throat. "We can take my car…"

She turned to him. "Do you mind if we walk? It shouldn't take that long. And it's nice out this evening. I told my family we'd just meet them there."

"Walking is always fine by me."

They walked in comfortable silence until her pace got slower the closer they got to the Montgomerys' beach house. Their house was nestled in with a line of other large rambling houses, directly on the beach. Well, not exactly nestled. Each house seemed a bit larger than the next one.

They walked up the long, curved drive and climbed the stairs to the front door. The door was opened by a uniformed man. "Good evening. Welcome." He motioned for them to step inside.

They entered, and Ben looked around at the rooms brimming with people. He looked down at his slacks and dress shirt. Not as snappy as some of the men here, but passable.

A server walked up to them and handed them each a glass of champagne.

"We might never find your family in this crowd." He looked around, scanning the faces.

"And that's a bad thing?" Her laughter tripped across the entryway.

They went to a room to their left where people were milling around looking at a handful of paintings placed in the room. He felt Charlotte freeze at his side. He looked in the direction she was staring and saw a delightful painting of a beach scene. A man and a dog— who he swore looked like Noah McNeil and his dog Cooper—played fetch by the waves. He stared at the small artist card in the corner.

Charlotte Duncan. Local Artist.

He turned to stare at her. "That's your work?"

She nodded silently.

She never ceased to amaze him. She was a *very* talented artist. The question was, why was she here with *him*? He was just a boat mechanic. Okay, he ran the marina, too. Managed their chain of marinas. But still, he didn't seem her type. "It's *wonderful*. You didn't tell me it would be on display here."

"I… I thought it would be tucked back in some corner. Not right out here in the first room everyone passes by when they come to the house." Her voice was a whisper.

"You must be so proud." He squeezed her arm.

"I'm… terrified."

"Charlotte, there you are. It figures you'd be late." She turned to see her sister and parents standing in the doorway to the front room. "I know it's fashionable to be late… but really? You were supposed to meet us here at seven." Eva swept into the room, her parents trailing behind her.

Ben looked at Eva and smiled. Of course. Now he had the woman he really wanted to be here with.

"What *are* you wearing? Where is that

gorgeous dress Mom picked out for you?" Eva frowned.

Charlotte tried to get out some words. Any words.

"And what were you two staring at?" Eva turned to glance at the painting and walked over to inspect it. She whirled back around toward Charlotte. "You did that?"

She nodded.

Eva's eyes widened in surprise. "But that's not the style of painting you do. Your work is... impressionistic. Marketable. This is just so... nostalgic. It isn't... well, not the kind of painting a person would want hanging in their home. It's not *artwork*. Why on earth is it on display here at the Montgomerys' house?"

At that very moment, Camille entered the room, along with Delbert. "There you all are." Camille smiled welcomingly at Eva and their parents, ignoring Charlotte. "I see you've found Mama's art display. She does so love to show some artwork at her parties. Paul Clark sets it up for her. She's quite a patron of the arts."

Eva nodded toward the painting. "That's Charlotte's."

Camille walked up close to it and frowned. "Well... isn't that... ah... *nice*?"

135

Delbert stepped forward. "I love this painting. It's so real and emotional." He turned to her, and she realized she still hadn't said a word, so she just gave him a weak smile.

Delbert turned to her parents. "You must be so proud of her. Are you all going to still be around for the local artist show next Friday? I hear Charlotte will have some work shown in it."

"No, I'm afraid we're leaving on Sunday," her father said.

"That's a shame. I'm sure it's a thrill to see your daughter's artwork in a gallery."

Eva stepped forward. "She used to do *real* artwork. I'm not sure why she'd be doing paintings like this." The disdain was clear in her voice.

Charlotte took a deep breath, fighting against the anger surging through her. The anger won.

She whirled around to face her sister. "Because I *like* doing these paintings. Working on these paintings is the first time I've come alive in a long time. *And* I need the money. I'm broke."

She heard her mother gasp and look around

the room to see who was hearing her daughter's outburst.

"How can you be broke? You sold really well in L.A. and had some other national showings." Eva frowned. "Why turn to this?" She flung her hand toward the painting.

She squared her shoulders, anger gurgling to the boiling point. "I like painting these scenes. Yes, they are different than my other work, but they are... They fulfill something deep inside me. They are the first work I've been happy with in a very long time."

"So... you just spent up all your money?"

"Sh... girls," her mother interrupted.

She ignored her mother's warning. "No, I didn't spend it all. Worse. I let my agent, Reginald, trick me out of it. And now he's left the country, so that is that. Now I need to start earning again. I'm going to do more of these paintings and have an exhibit at Paul Clark's gallery here on the island. *And* I'm going to paint furniture to sell at Bella's shop on Oak Street."

Eva flicked her perfectly curled hair behind her shoulder. "You're going to paint *furniture*?"

"Yes, if Bella will take my work on

consignment." She paused, surprised to find that Ben still stood by her side.

"Well, you should be really proud of this work," Del interrupted, obviously trying to smooth things over.

Eva ignored him. "You just need to quit messing around and get a real job."

"And you should quit telling me how to live my life." She stood in front of her sister, anger and resentment rushing through her. "I'm done with it. Art makes me happy. I love these paintings I'm doing now. And I love doing the furniture, too. I'm hoping to make enough to live off of. I don't need much. And it's too bad if you don't approve because I just don't care."

Eva finally looked around the room and everyone staring at them. "Sh! Keep your voice down. No one wants to hear your problems," she hissed.

Her father stepped up. "I think we should table this discussion for another time. How about we go out and get some Chardonnay for you ladies?"

She stood and stared at her father for a long moment. "And another thing. I *hate* Chardonnay. Always have. I've told all of you that a million times, but you just don't listen to me." She turned around on her heels and stalked out of the room, passing by Delbert who gave her a surprisingly supportive look, and Camille—whose look wasn't supportive at all.

She nodded at Camille as she walked past. "*Great* party."

Then she passed by Eva who was glaring at her, shaking her head, and her mother who looked mortified. She didn't say another word to either of them.

CHAPTER 16

Charlotte rushed outside, into the fresh night air, and hurried down the driveway. Away from the Montgomerys' monstrous beach house. Away from Eva's cruel words and her mother's dismayed face.

And away from the offered glass of detested Chardonnay.

She turned at the sound of someone hurrying up behind her and paused. Then frowned. "Ben, what are you doing? I'm fine. I'm just going to walk back home."

"You came with me, I'll see you home."

"No, that's okay. Go back in. Go on after her."

"After who?"

"Eva. I'm sure she needs someone to calm

her down now that I finally got the nerve to stand up to her. She looked... very ticked off."

"Why would I want to go after Eva?" His forehead wrinkled.

"Because you've always had a thing for her. I'm sure you'd rather be with her than walking me home."

"I—well, maybe in high school I had a silly crush. Most of the guys did." He shrugged. "But I don't want to go after Eva." He reached out and took her hand. "Charlotte... I'm interested in *you*. I want to take *you* out."

It was a good thing he was holding firmly onto her hand because she might have fallen if he didn't steady her. "You... what did you say?" Her heart pounded in her chest. And not from the confrontation with her family.

"I said I want to ask you out. I mean, I'm asking you out. Will you go out on a date with me?"

"A date?" She couldn't quite comprehend what he was saying. This night had been a whirlwind of surprises and she couldn't catch her balance.

"Yes. How about Sunday night? We could go to Magic Cafe for dinner. Or anywhere for that matter. I just want to take you out."

"On a date?" She knew she was repeating herself.

He grinned then. "Yes. A date. You know, where two people go to the same place. Maybe have something to eat. Talk a bit. Get to know each other better. You've heard of them."

She smiled then. "I've heard of them."

"So… is that a yes?"

"Yes, it's a yes."

"Perfect. Now how about I walk you home? We could crack open a bottle of red wine… I hear you don't like Chardonnay." He grinned again.

She threw back her head and laughed, letting the feeling sweep away her anger at her family and wrap her up in this surprise date request from Ben. "Sounds perfect." She tucked her hand in the crook of his arm, and they slowly made their way back toward their bungalows.

Ben suddenly stopped. "Hey, I have a better idea. How about we go aboard Lady Belle? It's a beautiful night. We can sit on her and watch the bay and the stars."

"I'd like that." It did sound peaceful. She needed some peace. Her mind was still reeling from the events of the night. She knew she would pay the price with her family for making a scene at the party, but she didn't really care. It had been long overdue, and Eva had been... impossible.

Ben led Charlotte to the marina and down the long dock to the end slip. They climbed aboard Lady Belle. Charlotte settled down on a cushioned seat while he slipped inside to grab some wine.

He couldn't get the look on Charlotte's face out of his mind. The look when Eva had torn into her in a mean-girl style he hadn't seen in action since high school days. But he'd been so surprised and proud when Charlotte stood up to her and held her own.

He couldn't imagine having a family that never supported you. His parents had always supported him and his brother and the choices they made. Even when his brother chose to leave and take a job up in Michigan, they'd supported him.

He couldn't remember Charlotte's parents ever being supportive of her. His mind flashed back to a high school art show. Charlotte had won first place at the show, and he remembered her standing alone when the principal announced the winner. Her parents had been nowhere around, even though many other parents had been there to cheer their children on.

But they'd been there when Eva had been recognized for making the highest SAT score and when she'd been crowned Homecoming Queen.

He scowled and dug out two nice wine glasses. He put the wine and glasses on a tray, grabbed a light throw blanket, and headed back outside.

Charlotte looked at him and smiled when he came out. She'd kicked off her shoes and tucked her legs up under her skirt.

"Getting unwound?" He settled beside her and poured the wine.

She took the offered glass. "Trying to. It was quite a night. I'm sorry you had to see that scene between my family and me. I don't usually do those kinds of things in public." She laughed. "Who am I kidding? I don't usually do that in private, either. I'd gotten so I just always let them have their say. It seemed easier that way. But tonight... well, it was just too much."

"They're wrong, you know."

"About what?"

"Everything. Your outfit is stunning… *you* look stunning. And your artwork is wonderful. You're very talented."

She blushed in the moonlight. "You're like a one-man cheering section."

"And everything I said is the truth." He reached over and brushed a lock of hair away from her face. "And I have another truth for you."

"What's that?" She looked up at him.

"I want to kiss you."

Her eyes widened. "You do?"

"I do. Do you think that would be okay?"

"I think… I think it would be… a good idea."

He lowered his lips to her and kissed her slowly, gently wrapping a hand around her neck and pulling her close to him.

She sighed.

He growled and deepened the kiss. When he finally pulled away her eyes were dreamy and her cheeks a rosy pink color. He draped the blanket around them and pulled her close to his side.

"I have a truth, too," she said quietly,

looking down at her hands, then back up to him.

"What's that?"

"I want you to kiss me again."

"This truth-telling is working out really well." He grinned and did as she asked.

CHAPTER 17

Charlotte woke up early the next morning and stretched lazily. Then the memory of last night's blow-up at the Montgomerys' party came back in full force. She frowned. But just as quickly as the memory of the party assaulted her, the lovely memory of sitting on the boat with Ben overcame it.

Ben's kind words.

Ben's kisses.

The enchanting night with moonlight and stars. They'd talked for hours, then he'd finally walked her back to the bungalow.

She jumped out of bed, a smile on her face, and headed to the kitchen for coffee.

"Morning." Robin handed her a steaming

cup of coffee then stood and eyed her skeptically. "What's up?"

"What do you mean?"

"You're *smiling* and it's only seven a.m."

"I had a fabulous evening."

"At the party? Did you meet any interesting people? Did everyone love your painting that Paul put on display?"

She held up a hand. "I did not meet any interesting people. No, not everyone loved my painting."

Robin frowned. "And yet, you're smiling."

Charlotte slipped into a kitchen chair. "I *am* smiling."

Robin sat across from her. "So, tell me the rest."

"I had a huge blowup with my family. At the party. In front of... well, a lot of people."

"You did?"

"I'd tell you that Eva started it... but that sounds so childish."

"But she did, right?" Robin grinned.

"She did." Charlotte laughed. "And I'd had enough. She started with the stupid dress they bought that I didn't wear then moved on to criticizing my painting."

"And how did that go for her?"

"I stood up to her. And I shocked her with my idea of doing painted furniture on consignment. And I told her I was broke. I guess the whole town knows I'm broke by now because I wasn't exactly speaking quietly when I told her off."

"Good for you." Robin's eyes shone with pleasure. "High time you put Eva in her place."

"Mother was mortified. Then Dad tried to smooth things over by saying we should all go and have a glass of Chardonnay and calm down."

Robin threw her head back and laughed, her brown hair tumbling around her shoulders. "Bet that went over well."

"Let's just say I'm pretty sure they all will now remember that I hate Chardonnay." She grinned at her friend.

"That does sound like a great night."

"There's more."

"Spill it." Robin leaned forward, forearms on the table with her hands wrapped around her mug.

"Ben and I went back to his boat after all that. It turns out he's not interested in Eva. He's interested in *me*."

"Of course he is. He even was in high school."

"No, he had a crush on Eva."

"No, he was star-struck by Eva. Every guy was. But he didn't like her. He liked you. Don't you remember he even came to see the art show where you won that blue ribbon?"

She frowned. "He was there?"

"I don't think *he* even knew he had a crush on you back then. I could tell he liked you though. You're so much more his type than Eva. Plus… you're a nice person, which is more than I can say about Eva."

"Maybe…"

"So… you went back to his boat, and…?"

"We had wine and talked and… He's a good kisser."

Robin slapped the table. "Ha. Knew it. He does like you."

"He asked me out on a date. We're going out tomorrow evening after my family leaves." She sighed. "And I need to go over to the inn and at least talk to them today. If they're speaking to me. I'm not sorry about anything I said to them, but I am sorry it happened at the party."

"I don't think you have anything to apologize for," Robin defended her.

"I'm not going to apologize. I'm just hoping to have a civil conversation with them. Make sure they understood I was serious and that things are going to change between all of us."

Robin rolled her eyes. "Good luck with that."

Charlotte decided to head over to the inn after fortifying herself with copious amounts of coffee and a big breakfast. Or maybe she'd just been stalling. She looked around the perfectly picked up kitchen—she'd even mopped the floor—then neatly hung the kitchen towel on the handle of the dishwasher.

She quickly dressed in shorts and a t-shirt that said *Make a Wish Upon a Shell - It Really Works* and slipped on some flip-flops. She pulled her hair into a ponytail. She might get criticized for this outfit too, but it was comfortable and she planned on cutting across the island and walking up the beach to the inn.

She grabbed her sunglasses and one of her many hats and headed outside into the sunshine.

She glanced over at Ben's bungalow. His car was there, but he'd probably walked to work. He was a walker to everywhere, just like she was. One more thing they had in common.

A smile slipped across her face as she thought of last night on Lady Belle. With light steps, she cut across the island and walked down to the water's edge of the gulf. Families were camped out under pop-up umbrellas and children ran and squealed, letting the waves chase them up the shore. A couple of grade-school aged kids were busy flying kites, each one trying to see if they could make their kite go the highest. Just a lovely, typical Saturday on Belle Island.

Of course, just about everything seemed lovely to her today. Except for the whole going to talk to her family...

She walked up the shoreline until she reached the inn, then rinsed her feet in a faucet near the steps and slipped on her flip-flops. She climbed the stairs and entered the inn. Sara waved to her from across the room and hurried up to her.

"How was the party at the Montgomerys'?"

"Eventful. I'll tell you the whole story, but first I need to find my family."

"I was just talking to Aunt Lil, and she said your family just finished with a late breakfast and were headed back to their cottage. She also said they were checking out early and heading back home today. I thought they were staying until Sunday?"

Charlotte frowned. "I did, too."

"Yes, they said something about needing to get back early."

She shook her head. She knew why they *needed* to get back early. They were escaping any fallout from her outburst at the party.

And they hadn't said a word to her about leaving early. Were they just going to text her after they left and say they were gone? Not even say goodbye?

"Thanks, Sara. I better go talk to them." She spun around and headed off toward the cottage they were staying in. She'd catch them before they had a chance to leave. She wouldn't apologize, but she hoped to at least smooth things out between all of them.

Or not.

Charlotte knocked on the door of the cottage.

155

Eva flung open the door but just turned away when she saw it was her. Charlotte stepped into the cottage, uninvited. "I heard you were leaving today."

Eva whirled back around to face her. "We are. You ruined our vacation. And it's so embarrassing. We'll never be able to come back to the island again."

"Pretty sure you're exaggerating just a bit."

Her mother entered the room carrying a tote bag and paused when she saw her. "Oh, Charlotte."

"Hello, Mother. I hear you're leaving early."

"Your father needs to get back."

"Really?" She didn't believe that at all.

Her mother set her bag down on a chair and turned to face her. "I'm so disappointed in you. All that commotion and embarrassment at the Montgomerys' party. It was... well, it was disgraceful. I raised you better than that."

"But Eva is allowed to say whatever she wants about what I wear, what I do for a living, and criticize my paintings? That's how you raised *her*?" She was not going to stand here and let her family blame her for their early departure.

"Don't be impertinent." Her mother frowned.

Her father entered the room, pulling a large suitcase behind him. "Oh, Charlotte. I was just getting ready to call you and tell you the girls have decided we'll leave early. Too bad, too. Had a golf game scheduled for this afternoon."

She shot an accusing glance at her mother, but her mother just looked down and fiddled with her tote bag.

"I was hoping we could talk before you go. I meant what I said that things need to change between us." She stepped further into the room.

"Let's not get into it all again. We do need to get back. Besides, I couldn't bear to show my face on the island now. Not after that scene you made. And it was so embarrassing apologizing to Camille for you." Eva let out a long put-upon sigh.

"You didn't need to do that."

"Of course I did. It was terrible. You ruined their party."

"I doubt it ruined their party." She rolled her eyes.

"Well, it was very unfortunate. We left soon after you did. I could feel all the people there staring at us." Her mother shook her head.

"I'm sorry you felt you had to leave early, and I probably could have chosen a better time to stand up to Eva... and to all of you. But, Eva, your remarks were cruel and uncalled for. I don't tell you how to run your life... or what to wear... and you have no right to tell me what I can and can't do. I'm tired of your constant remarks criticizing me and belittling me. I'm an adult. I make my own choices."

"Poor ones," Eva muttered.

"This arguing is giving me a headache." Her mother rubbed her temples. "Charlotte, just drop it. But I was very displeased with your actions at the party."

Let's just drop it, but first her mother had to get in one last dig? And didn't it take two people to argue? She turned to her father. "Dad?"

He looked at her for a long moment. "I listened. I heard you. And let's just say I won't forget that you don't like Chardonnay, that's for sure. But your mother has a headache and I should get the car packed."

She stood staring at her family. Wondering how she could have ever been born into this family, how she could be related to them. There was not going to be any smoothing things over, no more talking. That was clear.

"Okay, then. Have a safe trip." She spun around and walked back out the door and hurried down to the beach, once again speeding away from Eva, from her family. Things were never going to work out with them.

She suddenly felt like an orphan. A woman without a family. But maybe being estranged from her family wasn't necessarily a bad thing if they were going to be so poisonous to her mental well-being.

She stood at the edge of the sea, letting the waves lap at her ankles. And for all the world, she felt like a little lost child.

Then as she stood a while longer, a peace settled over her. Her jangled nerves soothed. Her pulse steadied.

She was proud of her stance with her family. And if they didn't want to accept her how she really was… that was their problem.

She only needed to accept herself.

CHAPTER 18

Paul peeked out the door and saw Josephine sitting out on the back deck. He hadn't meant to be this late coming home from the gallery, but he'd been busy getting ready for the local artist show.

He dropped some paperwork on the table and opened the door to the deck. He was rewarded with a smile from his beautiful wife. He still couldn't believe how lucky he was that he'd found her again.

He walked over and pressed a kiss to her forehead. "Sorry, I'm late."

She laughed. "You're always late when you're getting ready for a show. I don't mind. I've just been sitting out here enjoying the evening."

He slipped into the seat beside her on the glider and wrapped his arm around her shoulder. "I do like coming home to you."

She leaned against him. "We have a very good life."

"That we do, my love."

"Are things all set for Charlotte to join the show?"

"Pretty much. I think she does excellent work. Very distinctive style. Very emotional." He frowned. "I've heard some rumors about her ex-agent. People in the art community talk. She's well rid of him, but I'm sure it's hard for her to start over without an agent. Anyway, I want to help her out."

She smiled at him. "You're always looking to mentor an artist in need. Just one of the many things I love about you. You have a big heart." She patted his chest.

He caught her hand and pressed it to his lips.

"So, did you get Charlotte's work all arranged?"

"Almost. The paintings are there, but I'm not sure of the order that I want to hang them. Think you might drop by tomorrow and give me your opinion?"

"I'd love to. And anything else you need me to do this week, just let me know. I've taken care of ordering some appetizers and we'll have champagne, of course." Jo's eyes twinkled. "Champagne just makes these shows more festive, don't you think?"

"I think I'm lucky to have you to help me. You have made the openings of the shows more like a celebration. Plus, I love having you there with me."

She reached over and touched his face. "My dearest, Paul. There is nowhere I'd rather be."

He covered her hand with his own.

"My Jo."

CHAPTER 19

B en snuck in the back door to the kitchen at the inn and swiped one of Jay's cinnamon rolls.

"I saw that." Jay stood by the counter with a t-shirt on that proclaimed *A day without coffee is like... I don't know—it's never happened.*

"Feed the starving bachelor. Isn't that what you always say?"

Jay brought him a steaming mug of coffee. "If you're going to eat up the profits, you might as well have some coffee, too."

"You know I always offer to pay."

"You know Lil won't accept it."

He perched on a stool near where Jay was busy making another batch of cinnamon rolls.

"I heard the Montgomery party had a bit of

a kerfuffle." Jay reached for a large jar of cinnamon.

"How did you hear about it?"

"Robin. Charlotte told her."

"Well, it was impressive to see Charlotte stand up to her family."

"Robin said that Eva can be quite the mean girl when she wants to."

"She can. And she was toward Charlotte. I guess Charlotte had just had enough."

"We all get pushed to our limits sometimes." Jay's head bobbed in agreement.

"But I've got other news."

"What's that?"

"I'm going to take Charlotte out on a date tonight."

Jay grinned. "I already knew that, too."

"Is nothing secret in this town?" He laughed a good-natured laugh.

"Not if Charlotte tells Robin and... well, you know how it goes." Jay shrugged. "So, you're going to Magic Cafe? Good choice. I'm deeply hurt that you didn't come here, though."

"What? No, I just thought—"

"I'm teasing." Jay shook his head. "You can't take a little teasing?"

"I have to admit, I'm a little nervous. I haven't been on a date in forever."

"Like years."

"Well, neither have you," he shot back.

"Too busy."

"Same here." He took the last bite of his cinnamon roll. "But I want to take Charlotte out. Spend more time with her. She's interesting, talented, funny and not hard on the eyes, either."

Jay motioned to a tray of rolls, and Ben walked over and snagged another one. "It's kind of silly to be nervous. I mean, she's really easy to talk to. We have a good time together. It's just that calling it a date makes it official or something."

"You'll be fine."

"Maybe. Unless I do or say something stupid. I'm afraid she's a little fragile after that mess with her family."

"Fragile? I'd say it took a very strong woman to stand up to her family like that."

He chewed his lip. "It did. It was impressive."

"So you just need to relax and enjoy yourself."

167

"You're right." He took a bite of the recently retrieved cinnamon roll.

"I'm *always* right." Jay nodded somberly but as he turned around a grin crept across his features.

~

"You look great." Robin nodded her head in approval.

Charlotte looked in the mirror. "I feel like you're always getting me dressed these days."

Robin laughed. "It's not like you go on a date every day. This is *big*. Special."

She ran her hands down the side of her chambray skirt. She'd topped it with a simple white t-shirt and a silver necklace with tumbled turquoise. She turned this way and that and sighed.

"Okay, maybe you should French braid my hair this time. We're eating at Magic Cafe and I bet we'll eat outside. The wind is picking up, and the braid will hopefully stop my hair from going crazy."

"Good call. Sit."

She sat in a chair while Robin brushed then braided her hair. She stood and looked in the mirror again. "I think I need earrings." She walked over to her dresser and grabbed a pair of dangling silver ones and slipped them on her ears.

"You look perfect," Robin said.

"I still can't believe he asked me out. I mean on a real date. I'm not anything like his type. Like Eva."

"Thank goodness." Robin scowled. "And Eva is not his type. I just don't see Ben putting up with her sharp tongue."

"She is beautiful, and she is very successful."

"She's mean." Robin turned and walked out of the room. She called back, "You coming?"

After one last look in the mirror, Charlotte grabbed a small purse and followed after Robin. The doorbell rang, and she went to answer it.

Ben stood in the doorway with a bouquet of yellow flowers in his hands. "You look great." His eyes shone with admiration.

She'd take the flowers *and* the admiration. She reached out for the bouquet. "Come in. I'll put these in water."

She went to the kitchen, grabbed a simple mason jar vase, and placed the flowers carefully in it. She brought them back out and set them on a small table against the wall. "Thank you. They're very pretty."

"Well, buying you flowers told me one thing."

"What's that?"

"I don't know your favorite flower. But I think your favorite color is blue."

"You're right on the blue, and my favorite flower is a hydrangea."

He smiled at her. "I'll remember that for next time."

Her heart skipped a beat at the next time remark. He was already planning a next time?

She turned to Robin. "I won't be late."

"Hey, be as late as you want."

She and Ben walked outside. He turned to her. "Walk or drive?"

"Walk."

He smiled. "Good choice. My motto is, when the weather is good, always choose walking."

They wandered down the sidewalks toward Magic Cafe. The fronds on the palms waved in the breeze and white fluffy clouds drifted in the sky.

"I bet we're going to have a gorgeous sunset." She looked upward.

"Bet so, too."

Ben took her arm as they walked up the steps and into Magic Cafe. Tally waved to them and motioned them to come over to a table by the sand with a front-row view of the beach.

"Ben, Charlotte, great to see you," Tally greeted them.

"Hey, Tally." Charlotte hugged her.

He held out a chair for her and she slipped into it.

"What do you want to drink? And I'll send a waitress over."

"Red wine for me."

"I have a new cabernet. Dry with a hint of cherry flavor."

"Sounds perfect." She settled into her chair and kicked her shoes off under the table, burying her feet in the cool sand.

"I'll have the same." Ben sat by her side, both facing the ocean view.

He laughed when he glanced down at her feet. "Shoes off, huh?"

She grinned. "Your motto might be always choose walking. Mine is never miss a chance to have your feet in the sand."

The waitress brought their wine, and they

ordered their meals. Grouper. Blackened for Ben and grilled for her.

She added loving grouper to the growing list of things they had in common.

"So did you get a chance to clear things up with your family before they left today?" Ben leaned back in his chair, relaxed.

"They left yesterday. Evidently, according to Eva, I ruined their vacation."

"I thought you were impressive standing up to her."

"Also, according to Eva, they can never set foot on the island again. It was all too embarrassing."

"Their loss." He shrugged and took a sip of his wine.

"I'm thinking I won't be getting a bunch of texts this year like usual, commanding me to come to Austin for Christmas."

"Then you can have Christmas here."

"I haven't been here for the holidays in years. I guess I'll just see what the next months bring." It might be interesting to see Christmas here on the island again.

"And you have your paintings at Paul's gallery this week. Are you excited?"

"More nervous." She just hoped they sold.

Any of them. Just to bring in some cash. And if she could get ahold of Bella, then this week she would work on a few pieces of furniture for Bella's shop. Maybe things could turn around for her. At least she didn't have the stress of her family in town now.

The meal ended all too quickly as far as she was concerned, and they slowly walked back to Bayside Bungalows.

They stood awkwardly on her porch and she didn't know if she should ask him in, or kiss him, or what.

"I... I better go. Really early morning tomorrow."

She should ask him in.

Or kiss him. She wanted to kiss him.

He leaned over and gave her a quick kiss. Not exactly the type of kiss she'd been thinking of...

He smiled at her and with a little wave, he headed across the courtyard to his bungalow.

Next time she'd speak up quicker and invite him in.

Or she'd kiss him like she wanted to be kissed...

CHAPTER 20

C harlotte clicked off her cell phone the next morning and set it on the counter. She'd just spoken to Bella who was excited to put some pieces of furniture in her shop. Charlotte was going to hit up Goodwill and a local antique mall and see if she could find some pieces for a low cost that might work. Bella mentioned that teal colored furniture was selling well and also nautical themed pieces with anchors or compass stencils on them.

She wanted to finish the pieces as soon as possible, so maybe she'd get some money coming in. That along with working on redecorating the two rooms at the inn should tide her over for a while. Robin had offered to pay the full rent for a month or so if things got tight, but she didn't want to do that.

She grabbed her phone again and searched for places to shop on the map app. She quickly made a list. The best shops were on the mainland so she'd head there.

She grabbed her purse and keys and headed to the inn, hoping to borrow their van for her shopping expedition since she'd also be looking for a couple pieces of furniture for remodeling the rooms at the inn while she was out.

She hurried into the inn, looking for Robin or Lil to check on using the van. Lil was at the reception desk and Sara was chatting with her.

"Hey, Char." Sara waved.

"Morning. I was wondering if I could borrow the van. I'm headed to the mainland to do some shopping for furniture. I talked to Bella and she said I could sell some pieces at her shop and I want to get some for the remodel of the rooms here, too."

"Of course you can." Lil nodded.

"Mind if I tag along?" Sara asked.

"Not at all. Aren't you working today?"

"I worked on a presentation all weekend and I'd love to take a bit of time off."

"Perfect. I'd love the company."

She and Sara headed to the mainland and stopped at the first shop on her list. They wandered around and she checked on how sturdy a small table was and eyed a dresser with good lines, but she'd need to fix the drawer runners.

They bought a few pieces, a worker helped them wrestle them into the van, and they headed for the next shop.

"Hey, look, you're in luck. Thirty percent off if you spend over a hundred today." Sara pointed to the sign.

She swallowed at the thought of all the money she was spending today. The first shop's prices had been ridiculously low, which was great. She hoped this one was the same.

They wandered around and she found a desk, a few chairs, a coffee table, and a darling set of nightstands. She'd put them on her credit card and hoped something sold before the whole bill was due. She hated doing that, but she needed to invest in this to be able to earn something back. But she never put things on credit that she didn't have the funds to pay for. She stood in front of the nightstands, chewing her lip, and debating on not getting them.

"Let me buy this batch of furniture for you."

Sara offered. "Some of it will be for the inn, right? Then you can pay me back for what you sell at Bella's shop."

"I can't do that."

"Of course you can."

"No… I don't want charity. I made this financial mess, I'll get myself over it."

"Okay, then which pieces are for the inn. I'll buy those, at least. Then we'll still pay you for fixing them and painting them."

"The dresser from the last shop and these nightstands I think would work for the inn." She did the quick math. If Sara paid for those pieces, she'd almost have enough to pay off the rest. She'd just cut back on something.

Like eating…

They loaded up the furniture and Sara suggested they stop and get lunch at a place by the harbor before they went back to the mainland.

"I can't." She shrugged. She certainly didn't have funds for eating out.

"My treat."

"No… I can't."

"Charlotte, don't argue with me. We're eating at Harbor View and I'm buying."

"You're getting as bossy as Robin." She gave in with a small smile.

"I learned from the best."

They went to the restaurant and she ordered a small salad. They watched the boats go by in the harbor.

"Wow, look at that one. I swear it's bigger than our bungalow." She pointed at a huge yacht heading out of the harbor toward the gulf.

"Some people have more money than... well, than I don't know what." Sara shrugged.

"So how are things with you and Noah?" She turned from watching the boats. Or ships. When did a boat become a ship? She shook the thought away.

"Things are great."

"So you two are getting serious?"

Sara smiled. "Maybe. We've done some talking about the future, but nothing definite. It all seems a bit unreal to be dating him again. I can't believe we ended up together after all these years."

"You two were meant to be."

"How about you and Ben? I heard you guys had a date."

"We did. I had a great time. He's a good

guy. Funny. Nice. And we like a lot of the same things."

"You going to go out again?"

"I don't know. He hasn't asked me again."

"Hey, you know you could ask him out." Sara eyed her over the fish taco she was holding.

"I could, but… well, I want him to ask me." She shrugged.

Sara laughed. "I'm sure he will soon."

Unless he hadn't had as good a time as she had. He'd walked her home after Magic Cafe, kissed her once, then said he had an early morning and left.

"I don't know. Maybe we're just kind of friends or something. I just don't really know where I stand with him."

"Dating is awkward sometimes. Especially at first."

"I hate not knowing where I stand with him… or how out-of-control my life is now. *And* my finances in a mess."

"But you're working things out." Sara sent her an encouraging look. "Your paintings will be in the art show this week. Maybe one will sell right away. You're doing this furniture for Bella's shop. You're a strong woman and you're making your life turn around. I really admire you."

Charlotte basked in Sara's compliment. There was nothing like having friends like Sara and Robin. Nothing. Always supportive, always there for each other. "You know I love ya, right?"

"Right back at you, Char."

Ben decided to drop by his mom's house again to check on her. Okay, so he'd checked the community center's website and saw that the knitting club was meeting again today. He hoped his mom was going to go.

He walked into the kitchen and was pleased to see his mom packing up her knitting bag.

She turned to him. "You know, I'm perfectly capable of walking to the community center on my own. And I'm quite aware that you started this whole invite Ruby to the knitting club thing."

He put on his best innocent expression—not that it had ever worked for him with his mom. "What are you talking about?"

"Benjamin..." She waved a knitting needle at him. "I know what you're up to, but I'm fine. I like puttering around my house. I like to read and knit and just... Anyway, I'm fine. You should stop worrying about me."

He walked over and pressed a kiss to her forehead. "I do worry about you. I just want you to... be happy."

She looked directly at him. "I am happy, son. In a different way though. I miss your father. He was... my whole life. Well, you and your brother, too." She turned her back on him and kept rustling around in her knitting bag. "It has taken me a while to... adjust. It's hard to go to the marina now. So many memories. I expect to be standing on the dock and seeing him pulling one of his endless supply of boats in. But... that's not going to happen again."

"Mom, I'm sorry. I know you miss him."

"I know you miss him, too." She turned back to face him. "But life goes on, doesn't it?"

"It does. We have to learn to deal with both the blessings and the pain that life dishes out to us."

"That, we do. And I'm trying. But you know what? It's not your responsibility to fix things for me. I need to work it out on my own."

"Maybe you could join the book club at the community center, too."

"Ben, are you listening? I love you son, but

you're a fixer, just like your father. But sometimes a person needs to just work things out on their own."

"Sorry, I'll step back." He'd at least *try* to. But he only wanted to help...

She smiled at him. "Now, would you care to walk me to the community center?"

He grinned. "What a great idea."

CHAPTER 21

Charlotte stood in Paul's gallery on Friday evening, nervously waiting for the show to open. She chatted with a few of the other local artists. She especially enjoyed talking to the woodcarver. He'd carved a large blue heron that if she'd had the money she would have loved to buy.

She moved over and stood in front of the wall that held her paintings. Paul had chosen a mix of beach scenes and town scenes. He'd priced them higher than she thought they should be, but he insisted they were priced fairly. He knew better than she did. She'd always left that to Reginald. Not that that had turned out well.

If even one painting sold tonight, it would start to help her out of her financial mess.

Paul's wife, Josephine, was busy in the corner arranging a small table of hors d'oeuvres and glasses of champagne.

She glanced at the loose watch on her wrist, twisting it so she could see it clearly. One more minute.

She saw Paul head to the door, flip the sign to open, and unlock it. A few people were waiting to come inside. She swallowed, not sure why she was more nervous about this showing than big, fancy openings in L.A. and Chicago and Boston. This was just a small town in Florida, not an artist Mecca.

She made small talk with customers when they walked by her paintings, answering questions and smiling—always smiling.

"Hey, you."

She turned at the sound of Robin's voice. A familiar face. Excellent. "I'm so glad to see you." She threw her arms around her friend and hugged her close. Exactly what she needed. Moral support.

"Sara and Noah are over there grabbing some champagne. I told them to get one for you. You look like you could use it."

"I'm… a bit nervous."

"You look it. Just take a deep breath. Relax."

"That's easy for you to say. It's my first showing of work of this kind. Well, not counting the party, and we know how that turned out."

Noah and Sara walked up and he handed her a glass. "Quite a turn-out. Though the local artist show is always one of Paul's biggest draws. People love to see work from the locals. I put a notice about it on the community center website."

"Your display looks amazing." Sara stood in front of the pictures, carefully looking at each of them.

Paul came up to her with a huge grin on his face. He leaned in close to her and whispered. "You've already sold a piece. The gazebo one."

"I did? I sold one?" She couldn't keep the surprise out of her voice.

Robin and Sara spun around. "Ha, I told you." Robin looked triumphant.

"Yes. I was sure you would."

Paul smiled and turned around to greet some more customers.

"What's this I hear? You've already sold one?" Ben walked up to them looking spiffy in freshly pressed khakis and a light yellow button-down shirt that brought out the amber flecks in his brown eyes.

"You came." She smiled at him. She was finally surrounded by those she cared about all around her. They all turned out in support. Even if her family would never support her, her friends did. And Ben was a friend, right? Or what was he? She'd only seen him once this week, she'd been so busy. And that had been in passing at the inn when she'd been there looking for Sara and he'd been there to meet up with Jay. She pushed the thoughts away, unwilling to dissect their relationship on a night like tonight.

"Of course I did. Where else would I be on your big night?" He walked over to look at the paintings, then turned back to her. "These really are good. Very good."

She felt the heat of a blush creep across her cheeks. Before she could answer him, she turned at a light touch on her arm.

"Hello, Charlotte."

"Del, it's nice to see you."

"I try to always make it to opening nights of Paul's shows if I'm in town. He's an excellent judge of art." He looked at her paintings. "I see these fit in well with the tone of the painting I saw at Camille's mother's party. I really do like the style. Do you have an agent who's representing you now?"

"Not right now."

He nodded. "Let me know if you get one. I might have an opportunity for you if you're interested. Or I could speak to you directly."

She panicked then. What did she know about the financial side of selling her work? Reginald had always handled that for her. She hadn't dealt with any of the selling or arranging shows or arranging payment.

She took a deep breath, reminding herself that things were changing now and that she could handle it. She could handle everything, right? She was at least going to make a good attempt at it. "You could speak directly to me."

"Perfect. I'll call and set up a meeting." He smiled and headed over to look at another display.

"What was that all about?" Robin came up to her.

"I'm not sure. He said something about an opportunity."

Robin grinned. "See, I told you good things were going to start happening for you."

She felt her phone vibrate in the pocket of her skirt but ignored it. She needed to concentrate on the show, and she was riding a high. It felt so good to be showing her work again... not to mention selling.

She turned as an older couple came up and asked her if she'd painted the lighthouse on the point yet. She told them she had, but that painting wasn't here on display but would be in a few weeks when Paul was doing a full show of her work. They smiled and said they'd be back.

She talked to more customers and glanced at her watch, surprised it was almost time for the gallery to close. Where had the night gone?

Her phone vibrated again. Then again. She finally snatched it from her pocket, wondering who in the world could need her that badly that they kept calling. She wanted to just bask in this tiny success of hers.

She saw she had two voice messages and a handful of texts from her sister. She scrolled through the messages and her hand crept up to cover her mouth. Robin looked at her and hurried back by her side. "What's wrong?"

"It's my mom."

"What happened?"

She turned her phone for Robin to read the message.

·   ·   ·

Mom is in the hospital. Heart attack. It's your fault. See what you did when you caused all that stress for her?

"Oh, Char… it's not your fault. That's just Eva being Eva."

"I did cause a fuss. Mom was so upset."

"No, you stood up to them. You're allowed to do that." Robin squeezed her arm.

"I've got to go. Get a flight out." She looked around the gallery, trying to find Ben to tell him she was leaving.

"I'll drive you to the airport. Let's head back home, you can pack, and we'll find you the first flight out to Austin."

Sara hurried over. "You okay?"

"Her mom's in the hospital. I'm taking her to the airport. Will you tell Paul she had to leave?"

"Sure. And, Char, I'm so sorry about your mom."

She just nodded. She looked around the room, still looking for Ben, but couldn't see him. She didn't have time to track him down. She needed to get a flight and get to Austin.

"Come on, I'll drive you home. You can

search for a flight on your way." Robin grabbed her arm and led her out the door.

She hurried out of the gallery, tapping on her phone as she went, texting Eva that she was on her way, and looking for a flight.

CHAPTER 22

Lil looked up to see Sara and Noah climbing the stairs to The Nest. "How did the opening of the show go? I was hoping to get over to it but got tied up here at the inn. I'll be sure to drop by this week. Anyway, Jay finally chased me away from helping in the kitchen. I decided to humor him and come back here and watch the sunset and have a glass of wine. You two care to join me?"

"That sounds lovely." Sara grabbed a couple of glasses and she and Noah sat down on the glider.

"So tell me all about the show."

"It went well. I think Char ended up selling all her paintings. She'll be so excited when she hears that."

"She doesn't know?" She frowned.

"Char had to leave. She got a message that her mother was in the hospital. Heart attack. She grabbed a flight to Austin. Robin called and said she got Char to the airport. And Eva was texting her saying that it's all her fault since they had that family blow-up at the Montgomerys' party and her mother was so upset."

"Oh, I hope Charlotte doesn't blame herself. One upsetting moment doesn't cause a heart attack. It's genetics and diet and lifestyle."

"I'm sure Eva will do a good job on her and convince her it's her fault." Sara leaned back against Noah.

Lil smiled. She loved seeing her niece with Noah. He was a good man and made Sara happy. What more could she ask?

Sara looked at her and smiled. "I got lucky in the family department. Couldn't ask for a more supportive aunt."

"I got lucky in the niece department, too." A simple feeling of belonging swept through Lil. "And we'll have to convince Charlotte things are not her fault. Offer her our support."

"We will. She sure got stuck with a... not so nice family." Sara nodded.

"I'll make sure and mention her solo art

show when I send out the community center newsletter. We'll make sure she knows we support her." Noah dropped his arm around Sara's shoulder.

"I'll be sure to make it to her opening, too. I'll arrange work around it." Lil looked up at the sky, slowly turning yellow and orange.

Sara looked up, too. "Look, the first star."

"Make a wish, honey."

"I have everything I could ever want." Sara looked at Noah and he gave her a smile that was just for her.

Lil picked up her glass. "I feel that way, too. Especially now that my hip is healing. But I'm getting a bit tired. I think I'll leave you two to see the grand finale of the sunset."

"Night, Lil." Noah turned from staring at Sara.

"Night, Aunt Lil." Sara looked at her and then back at Noah.

Lil quietly slipped inside, really not a bit tired, but wanting to leave the two lovebirds to watch the sunset and have some time alone.

CHAPTER 23

The best connection Charlotte had been able to make was a red-eye that got her into Austin early the next morning. She'd tried to catch some sleep on the second leg of the flight but had only managed a little bit of fitful dozing.

She got to the airport and didn't want to bother her family, so she caught a cab directly to the hospital. She paid for the cab and got out at the front door of the hospital. She walked over to the information desk, and a very tired worker looked up at her.

"I'm looking for my mother. Isadora Duncan."

The worker typed in the name. "I'm sorry,

we don't have anyone admitted with that name."

"Can you check again?"

The worker typed in the info again. "Nope. No one by that name. Are you sure you have the right hospital?"

She tugged out her phone and checked the text messages from Eva. Yes, it was this hospital. This was the hospital her family always went to for any emergency. She frowned. Then a thought hit her... could her mother have... passed away? Her heart pounded in her chest. She didn't know how to ask the question.

"If someone comes to the ER and doesn't make it..."

The kind worker looked up at her. "Um... just a minute."

She tapped some more on her computer and looked up relieved. "No. You're good."

Maybe they'd sent her mother home? They didn't send someone straight home when they'd had a heart attack, did they?

She looked at the time, debating calling her family or just grabbing a cab to her parents' house. If they'd been up late with her mother, they were probably exhausted. She decided to grab a cab and headed to her parents' house.

She paid the driver, thinking of all the bills she was racking up. Last-minute flight. Two cab rides. Well, it couldn't be helped.

She walked up to the front door and paused. Ring the bell? Knock? She tried knocking first. No answer.

Her dad usually got up early and spent time in his study with his coffee and computer, checking the markets and news. If he wasn't too tired from last night, maybe she'd find him there.

She went around to the back of the house and saw the light on in his office. She knocked on the outside door to the office and he looked up in surprise. He got up and came to unlock the door.

"Charlotte, what are you doing here?"

"I came when Eva texted me about Mom's heart attack. I got here as soon as I could, but I had to get a connecting flight and it took all night. I went to the hospital, but they said she wasn't there."

He shook his head. "No, of course not. We came home last night. It wasn't a heart attack. It ended up she was having a panic attack."

Charlotte let go of the handle of her suitcase and sank into a chair, grateful and confused and angry at the same time. "A panic attack?"

"Yes, they determined quite quickly it wasn't a heart attack. Didn't Eva text you and tell you that?"

"No, she didn't."

"Maybe she thought we'd called you?"

Tears crept into the corner of her eyes, but she slashed them away, determined not to cry in front of her father. "I thought... I thought I caused her to have a heart attack."

Her father sat down in the chair across from her. "Nonsense. Your mother has been stressed out about a big benefit party she's throwing for the Ladies League. She isn't handling the stress of that very well. Eva talked her into going to the emergency room—which was the right thing to do because it *could* have been a heart attack. Similar symptoms. But thankfully, it wasn't."

"Thankfully." She swiped at one tear that escaped.

"And your mother might have been upset at the to-do at the Montgomerys', but she'll get over it. Eva exaggerated that it ruined our vacation. I, for one, had a splendid time seeing the island again and playing golf with my old buddies."

Charlotte stood. "I'm... I'm glad she's okay."

"How about some coffee and breakfast?"

"I think... well, I think I'll just head back home. I have a solo show coming up at Paul's gallery and I have a lot of work to do."

"But you just got here. At least go up and see your mother."

She let out a sigh. She supposed she should at least pop her head in and see her mom. At least Eva wasn't here.

"Come on."

She followed her father to the master suite. Her mother was sitting in bed.

"Look who came to check on you."

Charlotte followed in her father's wake.

"I'll leave you two to chat and I'll head back to my study."

"Charlotte, what are you doing here?" Her mother looked up in surprise.

"Charlotte was under the mistaken idea that you'd had a heart attack." Her father called back over his shoulder as he walked out.

Her mother blushed. "No, that was Eva's ridiculous idea. She got me all upset thinking I really was having a heart attack. Just a bit of a panic. The doctor gave me something to help with my stress level. You have *no idea* how stressful it is planning this big gala and benefit for the Ladies League."

"I bet." What else did she say to that?

"Anyway, I'm fine. Are you going to stay long?" Her mother frowned. "I don't have the guest room made up. I could probably call the maid service, but it's Saturday."

"Don't worry about it, Mom. Now that I know you're okay, I have to head back."

"Well, if you're sure." Her mother shrugged. That dismissive shrug that made Charlotte grit her teeth.

"Bye, Mom."

"Bye." Her mother looked back down at the magazine she was looking through.

Charlotte backed out of the room and went to find her father.

"I'm going to head out, Dad."

"You sure? You could stay a few days. Or longer if you want. You could always move back here for a bit and look for work. Get yourself back on your feet."

"Dad, I live on Belle Island. It's my home again. I love it there. I'm painting there… and my paintings are selling. Well, I sold one of them. Hopefully more when I have my solo showing."

He looked at her thoughtfully. "If you're sure. How about if you let me pay for your flight? That had to have cost you a pretty penny to catch a last-minute one."

As much as she would have loved to say yes, she didn't. She didn't want help from him or from anyone. "Thanks, Dad. But I've got it covered."

Just then the door swung open and Eva swept into the room. The thought occurred to her that Eva always *swept* into a room. Never just... entered it. And it bugged her. It bugged her a lot this morning in her exhausted-no-sleep state.

"I see you came to check on Mom. All the stress you caused her sent her to the hospital."

"Now, Eva, I think the stress she's not dealing well with is that big benefit she's planning."

"Charlotte and her episode at the Montgomerys' didn't help any."

"Eva... you know what? I'm—" She paused and took a deep breath. "I'm leaving now. And you can try to convince yourself that I'm the cause of all of Mom's problems. Heck, you can convince yourself I'm probably the cause of *your* problems. But you don't have to worry about that anymore, because I'm not coming back. Not to listen to you tear me down and tell me everything I'm doing wrong in my life. So you go on with your life. Have fun. I'm going back to Belle Island. To my friends. To my painting. To the life I love."

"Another tirade? Really?" Eva rolled her eyes. "And you're going back to *paint furniture*?"

"I'm going back to my *artwork*. And if you notice, I'm perfectly calm. Just telling you how things are going to be now." She turned to her father. "If you or mother would like to visit, you're welcome." She paused. "But only if you can accept me just as I am."

She turned, tugged on her suitcase, and went out the door. She got to the curb and realized she needed to call a cab or Uber or something. She pulled out her phone, eager to get back to the airport, find a flight, and get back to her real life.

And she wanted to get back to Ben. She definitely wanted to get back to Ben and sort out what was going on between them.

Charlotte pulled her suitcase—the one that had never even been opened—into her room back at her bungalow. Exhaustion came in waves. She'd been able to grab a couple hours' sleep on the flight back, but she was still running on empty. She headed to the kitchen to make some sweet tea.

If she could just stay awake for the day, she'd crash out early tonight and try to get back on schedule. She had a busy couple of weeks getting ready for her solo show. She had two paintings she wanted to finish up, and she was itching to start a brand new one. She wanted to paint the marina at sunset. And she needed to get over there and take some photos of it to work off of. It was just a bonus if Ben were there while she was taking her photos…

"Char? You here?" Robin came into the bungalow.

"In the kitchen."

Robin walked into her bedroom. "You look beat."

"I am. Exhausted. Angry. And I spent all that money on a trip where I wasn't even needed, much less wanted."

Robin hugged her. "I'm sorry, Char. But you're back here now where you belong."

Charlotte hugged her friend and looked around the bungalow. She did feel like she was beginning to belong here. For the first time in a long time, she felt like she was home.

She turned back to the counter. "Want some of my almost-famous sweet tea?"

"Sure do." Robin reached for a glass and got ice from the door of the fridge. "Then sit down and tell me all about your trip."

"It was… interesting. My parents were surprised to see me. Evidently they thought Eva had managed to tell me it was all a false alarm. Then I got to hear about how stressful it is running a gala."

Robin smothered a grin. "I'm sure it is."

"I am sorry my mom is stressed, but really? Then she seemed annoyed when she thought that I might stay a few days because she would have to call the maids to come clean and set up the guest room. Sometimes I think I live on a different planet than my family."

"Yes, you live on *our* planet. The one that Belle Island is on."

"You're right. I like where I am."

"And your paintings all sold at the show. That's fabulous news." Robin motioned toward the counter. "Oh, and Paul already wrote a check for you. It's over on the counter."

She jumped up and went to where Robin pointed. She opened the envelope carefully and pulled out the check. "Oh… wow." She stared at the number in awe.

Robin grinned. "So, it was a profitable evening?"

She whirled around. "I can't wait to deposit this. And now I don't have to worry about the rent, and I have enough to pay for all that money I wasted going to Austin."

"I'm happy for you." Robin looked smug. "I told you that you should show your work to Paul. You should always listen to me."

She laughed. "I should. And I usually do. You're too hard to argue with, anyway."

"Yep, that's my claim to fame." Robin took a long drink of her tea. "Though some people call it bossy."

She laughed again. "That, too."

CHAPTER 24

"Have you talked to Charlotte?" Jay stood by the oven, peering in at something that smelled wonderful.

Ben shook his head. He'd hoped she would call or text, but he hadn't heard a word. Hence, the visit to Jay this afternoon, hoping for information. But then, it didn't surprise him he hadn't heard from Charlotte. It was his own fault. He'd been such a goofball the night of their date. At the end of their date, he'd panicked, kissed her quickly, and ran back to his bungalow.

"Robin said she's headed back home today. It wasn't a heart attack like they first thought."

"It wasn't? That's good news." Relief washed through Ben. He'd been so worried when he'd missed her leaving the show last night. He'd heard why she left in such a hurry but wished he'd been able to help her or at least say goodbye.

They'd been missing connections all last week. And to be honest, he hadn't quite sorted out his feelings toward her, hence the panic the other night. Oh, he liked her. Had fun with her. But what did he have in common with a talented artist?

"The local artist show was a great success. Robin said all of Charlotte's paintings sold."

"I'm sure Charlotte will be thrilled. It was too bad she had to leave early." Ben shook his head. "But, of course, she needed to check on her mom after Eva said her mom was having a heart attack."

"She'll come back and get ready for her solo show. It will all work out." Jay walked over and perched on a stool beside him.

"So… you've only officially gone out with Charlotte once. You going to ask her out again?"

"Probably. I mean, yes." He raked his hand through his hair. "I got spooked a bit on our last date. Like what was I doing? What does she see in me? I... well, I kind of just fled back to the bungalow."

"So... ask her out again and figure out how you feel about her. Quit being such a goof."

Ben grinned. "You're probably right. I'll ask her out again."

"When?" Jay pinned him with a stare.

"Next time I see her."

"You know, they've invented this thing called a cell phone. You could call her..."

Charlotte walked into Paul's gallery later that afternoon, wanting to thank him for the check and having her at his local artist show. He looked up from where he was talking to a customer.

She waved and wandered around the gallery, giving him time. The door to the gallery opened and Delbert Hamilton entered. He lit up when he saw her. "Charlotte, just the person I wanted to talk to. Do you have a few minutes?"

"I'm all yours."

Del steered them to a corner of the gallery. "So, I have a proposal for you."

She looked at him. "What kind of proposal?"

"I've just recently purchased a small hotel on Moonbeam Bay."

"Oh, that area of Florida is beautiful."

"It is. A boater's paradise. They built a canal system with beautiful homes lining the canals with easy access to the harbor and the gulf."

She wondered what he was getting at, but let him talk.

"Anyway, I'd love some of your paintings to hang in the lobby of the hotel. They'd be perfect. And, if possible, I'd love to commission you to paint the old live oak in the town square there. It's near the harbor and the sunsets behind it are stunning."

"I... I don't know what to say." He wanted her work in his hotel *and* a commissioned piece?

"I drew up some papers. You can look them over. Talk to a lawyer if you'd like. It has figures on it. But it's negotiable if you don't think the payment is reasonable."

She glanced at the numbers on the paper he handed her and almost dropped the pages. "You're going to pay me this per painting, plus this for the commission piece?"

"Yes, if you agree." He gave her a warm

smile. "But you don't have to answer me now. Think about it. See if you feel the price is right."

As far as she was concerned, the price was wonderful. Fabulous. Perfect. But then she paused. She hadn't handled the money side of things. She should take her time and figure this all out. "Yes, give me a bit of time. But this does sound like something I'm interested in."

"Perfect. I'll be back in touch soon." He nodded to her, waved to Paul—still busy with his customer—and walked out of the gallery.

She stood there staring at the paper in her hand. Could the type of painting she was doing now really bring her this kind of money? And the commissioned painting? The amount Del was willing to pay for that kind of blew her mind.

Paul walked up to her. "You okay?"

"I… I think so. Del just made me an offer to do paintings for a hotel he bought on Moonbeam Bay."

"I heard he bought the old Cabot hotel. It's closed now, and he's remodeling it and doing some upgrades. He did such a great job on the Hamilton Hotel in Sarasota. I'm sure he'll do a great job with this one, too."

"I always had my agent handle the financial side of things. I'm unsure about all of this." She held out the paper to him.

Paul took it and skimmed through it quickly. "Reasonable offer, I think. And if your paintings keep selling well, he's getting quite a deal. They'll only go up in value. You really have a way of showing the emotion in your paintings. Of bringing a viewer right into your worldview."

"So, you think I should take the offer?"

"I have a lawyer I use for some of my work. Would you like him to look at the offer and contract?"

"Yes, that would be wonderful."

"With your permission, I'll give these to him and have him contact you. His fees are reasonable and he's a very sharp, level-headed lawyer."

"Thanks for your help, Paul. I feel a little out of my league with all this."

"You could get another agent to deal with this."

"I—I'm not ready for that, I don't think."

"Well then, I'll help you in any way I can."

"I appreciate that. You've done so much for me. The local artist show. My solo show."

"Oh, about your solo show. I've gotten some art critics to come to the opening. And someone from Florida Sunshine Magazine is coming to do an article for their art section. I've taken out some ads and done some promotion."

"Paul, I don't know how to thank you." Gratitude flowed through her.

He reached over and rested his hand on her arm. "Think nothing of it. I love helping you. And your show will bring in a lot of traffic to the gallery, so see, in a way, you're helping me."

The door to the gallery opened, and a couple walked in. "I better go see to them." Paul smiled and went over to greet them.

She stood there for a few moments trying to gather her thoughts. Things were spinning out of control in her life right now. But not in a bad way.

And suddenly she wanted to see Ben. Talk to him. Tell him everything that had happened. She whirled around, headed out of the gallery, and hurried down the sidewalk to the marina.

CHAPTER 25

Ben stood just outside the repair area of the marina. He'd finished up work on two boats today with the help of his other mechanic. He glanced at the sky full of fluffy white clouds. Looked like the makings for a beautiful sunset.

"Ben?" He turned at the sound of her voice, a smile already creeping across his face.

"Charlotte, you're back." He walked over wanting to take her hands but glanced down at his own. They still had grease on them from his day of working on the boats. He settled on just looking at her smiling face.

"I am back. And, if it's okay with you, I wanted to take some photos of the marina. I'd love to paint it at sunset."

"Fine by me." Especially if it meant she

hung out until sunset, which was a good hour or so from now.

"How about you start on some photos, and I'll go get cleaned up? Meet me back at Lady Belle when you're ready? I could round up some appetizers and we could wait for the sunset." Say yes. Say you'll stick around for a while.

"That sounds nice." She smiled at him.

A smile that warmed him and made him feel special. He caught himself right before he reached out to touch her face. She probably wouldn't appreciate a smear of grease on her rosy cheeks.

"Won't take me long to get cleaned up."

"Okay, I'll meet you at the boat."

He hurried away to Lady Belle and scrubbed up from his messy day. Luckily he kept some clean clothes on the boat. He'd been slowly moving his things aboard. His lease was up at the bungalow at the end of the month, and he planned on moving aboard by then.

He put together a cheese platter and sliced up an apple. Then he added some nuts to the side along with an assortment of crackers. He opened a bottle of red wine to let it breathe.

He quickly picked up around the boat, rinsing some dishes and straightening a stack of boating magazines. Glancing around, he decided he'd done all he could. He looked at his watch. Still a little bit of time before sunset.

"Ben?"

He hurried outside to help Charlotte board, eager to see her and talk to her. Or not talk. He didn't care. He just wanted to spend time with her. Figure things out.

And he wanted to kiss her again... without running away in a panic.

Charlotte settled on the seating at the stern of the boat. Ben disappeared inside and came back with a tray of food and a bottle of wine. Perfect. She wasn't very hungry and appetizers sounded like the perfect dinner as far as she was concerned. She'd take some photos, then head home to bed. Exhaustion was beginning to creep over her again and chase away the rush she'd had after all her excitement at the gallery.

Ben settled next to her. He smelled of outdoors and the faint scent of aftershave. He handed her a glass of wine. "To a beautiful sunset."

"To a great sunset." She raised her glass,

and they clinked glasses. She took a sip of the delicious wine, then set her glass down.

"So tell me how things went in Austin."

"Let's just say, not as expected. I wasn't needed, so I headed back." She really didn't want to get into the whole trip again. She wanted to put it behind her. "But I do have some exciting news."

He looked at her expectantly.

"Del Hamilton bought a hotel that he's remodeling on Moonbeam Bay. He wants to hang some of my paintings in the hotel and he commissioned a painting."

"That's great news."

"Paul's lawyer is looking over the contract and the offer. I always let my agent deal with the money stuff so I'm a bit unsure of it. But I'm determined to figure it out and handle it all myself." She could do it. She could. She'd just teach herself all she needed to know. No more letting someone else run things for her or make her decisions for her.

"I'm good at numbers if you need help," he offered.

"No, thanks. I've got it." She glanced at him and saw a hint of hurt in his eyes when she turned down his help.

"Okay." He looked away and took a sip of his wine.

"Ben... I..."

"Just wanted to put the offer out there."

"I appreciate it... but it's something I need to do myself." She changed the subject. "So what have you been doing recently? I haven't seen much of you."

"Well, let's see. Mom decided to join a knitting group at the community center. I'm glad about that. She's finally getting out of the house some. She's had a hard time since Dad died."

"I'm sure she has."

"Oh, and I finished up work on two boats. And I've decided to move aboard Lady Belle at the end of the month."

"Sounds like a lot has happened with you in just a few short days. So, you're moving here?" She would miss having him just a few bungalows away from her, not that the marina was more than a short walk away.

"Yes, it's been a dream of mine to live aboard a boat, and now that Lady Belle is all fixed up, it's time." He looked at her, then took her hand in his.

The warmth of his hand spread through her, connecting them.

"But I'll miss having you as a neighbor."

"I guess I'll just have to visit you here."

"Often." His eyes shone with anticipation. Then he leaned closer, tilted her face up, and kissed her.

A kiss that she wanted. Needed. It seemed like forever since he'd kissed her like that.

He finally pulled back. "Ah, that's what I needed."

She smiled. Sometimes their thoughts were so in sync it seemed like they were two of a kind.

CHAPTER 26

The next morning Ben was hard at work on his boat, hoping to get her finished and move aboard.

"Ben, are you here?"

He almost dropped the cloth he was holding to polish The Lady Belle's wooden door to the cabin. He must be hearing things because he swore that sounded like his mother's voice. But, of course, it wasn't. She never came to the marina anymore and would never come to Lady Belle. It held too many memories of his dad.

He frowned, set down the cloth, and popped out of the cabin to the back deck. Then he held onto the railing in surprise. "Mom?"

"Morning. I wanted you to meet my new friend, Mischief."

He knew his mouth was hanging open, but really, he couldn't be more shocked. "Mischief?" He stared at the dog at the end of the leash his mother was holding.

"Isn't he adorable? A bit of an imp, but so cute, right?"

"Are you walking him for someone?" He couldn't quite process this. His mother was *not* a dog person.

"No, he's my dog."

He gripped the railing with two hands now, trying to steady himself. "Your dog?"

"Yes, he needed a home. I heard about him at knitting club and went to go see him." She smiled and shrugged. "Next thing I knew he was coming home with me. We made a stop at the pet store for food, bowls, and things like that."

"Your dog?" He knew he was repeating himself, but how in the world did his mother end up with a dog?

She looked up at him and frowned. "Are you okay?"

He swung off the boat and went to stand by her. "I could say the same thing. A dog is a lot of work. We never had one when I was growing up. I thought you didn't even like dogs."

"Your father didn't like dogs. I do." She shrugged.

"Are you sure you're up to all the responsibility?"

"Ben, I'm not a child, and I'm not some feeble person. Quit treating me like one." She leaned down and petted the dog. "We have big plans for the day. We're going to meet Mary Lyons and Dorothy and go for a walk on the beach. Mary has a dog, too. Stormy. An adorable cavalier."

He should be happy that she was getting out and making friends. But a dog? He just didn't picture his mother as a dog person. *And* she'd come to the marina, and she'd come to Lady Belle.

He looked at her and decided to chance it. "You want to come aboard and see the changes I've made to Lady Belle?"

She looked at the boat for a long moment, a hint of sadness in her eyes. "Maybe next time. I'm sure Mischief and I will be back soon. We better run along now. Don't want to keep Mary and Dorothy waiting."

He watched while she walked back down the long dock, the dog trotting merrily by her side.

A dog. His mother had a dog. He just hoped

she could keep up with the dog because he sure wasn't going to take care of him for her. The last thing in the world he needed was a dog in his life.

Charlotte set down her coffee on the kitchen table when her phone rang. She glanced at it and frowned. The Desert View Art Gallery.

"Take it." Robin nodded from across the table.

She answered the phone. "Hello?"

"Charlotte Duncan?"

"Yes."

"You're a hard one to find. We've been trying to get in contact with you. We want to know your arrangements for coming to the opening of your show here in Palm Springs."

"My what?"

"Your solo show."

"I don't understand." She frowned, trying to follow the conversation.

"We've been trying to get ahold of your agent, Reginald. But he's not answering our calls. He set the show up a year ago. We book way in advance for the Palm Springs Festival of Arts week. It's a very coveted spot."

"I—he—didn't tell me about it. We've been —out of contact."

"Hm… we'd heard some rumors about him. But I had hoped since this show was set up so long ago that it wouldn't be a problem. I apologize for the late contact, but it took us a while to find a way to contact you directly."

"A solo show?" She still couldn't get over the shock. After all this time?

"We have the work ready to hang, and the brochure for the Palm Springs Festival of Arts has been out for months."

She couldn't believe she was finally going to have another shot at a big showing in a city known for supporting the arts. The Palm Springs Festival of Arts was one of the big draws to the area and a well-known art show. Having a showing in The Desert View Art Gallery that week would certainly get her name out there again.

She looked over and grinned at Robin. "This is exciting news."

"So, you'll still do it?"

"Of course." She gave Robin a thumbs up. This Palm Springs showing would put her back on top. Get her name going again after Reginald had stopped getting her new showings.

"Do you have a new agent who I should contact with the information?"

"Ah… no. Not yet."

"I will say that Michelle Isling was asking about your work."

Michelle Isling? Only one of the best agents in the business. "She was?"

"Yes, do you mind if I give her your contact information?"

"Ah… no. I mean, no, I don't mind. Yes, give her my information. That would be great."

"I'll give her a call. In the meantime, I'll send you the information regarding the show this afternoon. Why don't you give me your email?"

She gave her email address, clicked off the phone, and set it on the table.

"What's going on?" Robin raised an eyebrow.

"I finally got a good show. A really nice, *prestigious* one." She hopped up from the table and twirled around. "I've still got it."

"Of course you do."

She grinned and sat back down. "Things are finally starting to turn around for me. I'll do this show and maybe I'll get back on the circuit again. And Michelle Isling asked about me. She's like one of the top agents in the business."

"Does this mean you'll move back to L.A.?" Robin looked solemn.

"What? No. This is my home now. I mean... I might have to be gone some." She frowned. This is what she'd wanted for so long. Ever since Reginald had messed with her and stolen from her. It would be easier if she lived in California and got back into going to the parties and got her name out there again. And Michelle Isling! That was exciting.

She looked at her phone when it rang again. "Hello?"

"Charlotte?"

"Yes?"

"This is Michelle Isling. I just got off the phone with the curator from The Desert View Art Gallery. She said you aren't currently represented by anyone."

"I'm not."

"My firm would be interested in talking to you about representation. Do you have time to fly out and talk to us? All expenses paid, of course."

"Yes, I could make time." She grinned over

at Robin and mouthed the words Michelle Isling.

"Could you come this week? Say Wednesday?"

"Yes, that would work."

"Great, I'll make the arrangements and send you your flight information."

She set her phone on the table, staring at it. How had so much changed so quickly? She looked across at Robin. "She wants to represent me. I'm going there Wednesday to talk to her agency."

"That's great, Char. Great. I know this is what you've wanted." Robin stood, walked over to the sink, and placed her cup in it. "And if you think L.A. is where you need to be, I support you one hundred percent. But I'll miss you like crazy."

CHAPTER 27

Charlotte hurried over to the marina, anxious to tell Ben her good news. She almost skipped like a little kid along the town's sidewalks. Her own solo show. And in the middle of the Palm Springs Art Festival week. It didn't get much better than that for a relaunch of her name.

She found Ben working on Lady Belle. He stood on the back deck, his shirt off and his tanned chest and shoulders gleaming in the sunshine. His broad shoulders narrowed down to his lean waist. He turned around, and she tried not to stare at his well-defined abs.

"Charlotte, hi." He reached over for his shirt and snagged it from the railing. Unfortunately, he then slipped it on.

Oh, well, better to concentrate while she told him her news. "I have news."

He reached down a hand for her and she climbed aboard. "I have news, too."

"Okay, you go first." She was feeling bubbly and generous. Her news could wait.

"Mom did the craziest thing. You're not going to believe this, but my mother got a *dog*."

"She did? Good for her."

"Good for her? I don't think it's a good idea. It's so much responsibility. She barely gets out of the house to do anything. How can she take care of a dog when she's barely taking care of herself?"

"Maybe a dog is the perfect thing for her. I'm sure she's lonely all alone in that house. And she's not *old*, Ben. You're treating her like an old person. She's not. She's a young widow. And anyway, are you ever too old to have a dog? Maybe she wants the company. They're great companions."

"She's never owned a dog. What does she know about dogs?"

"Everyone is a first-time dog owner at one time." She didn't know why he was so upset about this.

"Well, I think it's a ridiculous idea." He shook his head. "What's your news?"

A wide grin spread across her face. "I got a solo show. In Palm Springs. At a really prestigious gallery."

"See, I told you your new work is great." He smiled.

"No, this is my *old* work. My agent set it up before... well, before we split. They have the paintings."

"But I thought you didn't paint like that anymore and you'd moved on to the type of painting you're doing now."

"I had. But... I'm sure I can still do my old impressionistic style. Now that I have a showing. Now that I have a chance again. And a big-name agent wants to represent me. I'm flying to L.A. on Wednesday to meet with her."

"California?"

"Yes, that's usually where L.A. is." She grinned at him, feeling alive with all her good news.

"Oh."

Oh? That was all he was going to say in response to her news? She looked at him expectantly.

"If this is what you want, then that is good news."

Her chest tightened. This was not the reaction she'd hoped to get from him. "It is what I want. I've worked a long time for this."

"Then I'm glad it's happening for you."

"So, do you want to go out tonight and celebrate with me?" She reached out and took his hand.

He stared down at her hand, then pulled away. "I'm sorry. I can't tonight. I've got a lot of work piled up."

She tried to hide the crestfallen expression she was sure was plastered on her face. "Okay, well, maybe after I get back from L.A."

"Sure." He picked up a cloth. "I better get back to work."

"Okay, I'll leave you to it." She climbed off the boat and walked away, slowly taking step after step away from him. Feeling more distant and more alone with every step.

Jay sat on a barstool at Lucky Duck, waiting for Ben to join him. His friend had called him this afternoon and practically begged him to come out tonight. He lifted a hand in a wave when he saw Ben come in.

Ben slipped onto the stool beside him and ordered a beer from Willie.

"So, what's up?"

"Oh, nothing much. Except my mom got a dog, for Pete's sake, and Charlotte is having a big art show in California. You know, all the way across the country."

Jay set his beer mug down. "Let's take this a step at a time. Ruby got a dog?"

"Yes, can you believe it? That's just crazy. She's never had a dog."

"She's probably lonely." He shrugged. "It will be good company for her."

"She can hardly take care of herself, much less an animal."

Jay looked at his friend. "Or... maybe it's that you've used the excuse of taking care of your mom for the last couple of years to avoid... well, avoid everything else. Dealing with the loss of your father, dating anyone. You've made your whole life revolve around taking over your dad's business and taking care of your mom. Now that she's getting more independent... maybe you're feeling a little lost yourself."

"It's not that…." Ben scowled at him. "Is it?"

"Something to think about."

"But… she's needed my help. For fixing things around the house. For dealing with her finances and dad's estate stuff. And to keep her company."

"Maybe she's decided it's time to take over her life again. Maybe she's stronger now. She gave herself time to grieve, and now she's ready to live again. Learn how to live without your father. She's young, Ben. She has a lot of life left to live."

Ben scowled again. "Since when did you get so smart?"

"It's my curse. What can I say? And now about Charlotte…"

"We were just beginning to get close. I think I might have feelings for her. Might. But now we won't have time to find out because she's going back to her fancy life in California."

"She's moving back?"

"I don't know. Maybe. It would make sense, wouldn't it?"

"You're such a dope sometimes." Jay rolled his eyes. "Tell her how you feel."

"I don't know how I feel."

Jay eyed him. "Of course you do. You're just afraid to admit it. Afraid of getting hurt. Afraid of… losing someone again." He took a sip of his beer. "And buddy, I think it's about time you dealt with your father's death."

CHAPTER 28

Charlotte opened her laptop and checked her email that night. She wanted to read the information about her solo show. The show that Ben had been decidedly *not* excited about.

She clicked on the email and downloaded the information. She quickly scanned it, then paused. She carefully read through it word for word.

Robin came into the room. "Thought I'd grab a beer, want one?"

"I... no... yes, sure."

"What's wrong?" Robin came over and handed her a beer.

"It's my solo show in Palm Springs. I got the date for it."

"When is it?" Robin plunked down beside her.

"The opening night is the *exact* same date my solo show opens at Paul's." She closed the laptop and took a sip of her beer. "And part of the deal of the solo show is that the artist comes for opening night. That's just part of how the Festival of Arts is run each year. All the participating artists know that. I knew that. I just didn't know the dates for it this year because I've been so out of that scene since I moved down here."

"Can't you just call and say you can't be there for the opening? Unless… well, if you want to be there."

"I even have a signed contract regarding the show. Only Reginald signed for me. That's why I knew nothing about it. He left without telling me."

"That's not good."

"No, it's not. Paul has done so much for me. I couldn't back out on him now. But this says I have a contract with them and I have to be there for the opening."

"It's something you've worked hard for. It could get you going again on your old style of painting. Get more shows booked."

She looked down at her hands. The hands that now painted a new style of art and also painted furniture. Not the artsy, impressionistic paintings she used to do. But... her old art *had* made her good money. And she needed money now.

How did everything get so complicated?

Robin eyed her. "So... what is that you really want to do? Contract and feelings of responsibility to Paul set aside?"

Robin had a way of doing that. Cutting to the heart of the matter. She gave her friend a weak grin. "That's the problem. I'm just not sure."

CHAPTER 29

Ben stood at Lighthouse Point early the next morning. Fog had spread across the bay earlier, but the light breeze off the sea had begun chasing it away. He looked up at the lighthouse, standing strong on the point. It used to guide the sailors safely home and into the bay.

He needed a lighthouse to guide him now. As Jay had so cleverly pointed out last night, he was being irrational about his mother and Mischief. He had to admit the dog was cute. And he could even grudgingly admit getting the dog had probably been a good idea. But he wasn't quite sure how he felt about his mother not needing him quite so much.

Things were changing so quickly for him.

He was used to planning his days around his mother's schedule. Making sure she was taken care of, that she had company, that things were taken care of with her home. He'd kind of made it his mission to take care of his mom ever since his dad had passed away.

Then there was Charlotte. She was going back to her famous artist life. He didn't fit in there. He hadn't even fit in at the Montgomerys' party. He'd never fit into the L.A. lifestyle.

And if he told her how he felt about her, would that hold her back? Would she stay here? Would she eventually resent staying here?

He laughed. He didn't even know how she felt about him, much less that she would stay.

And then there was his dad. A stab of pain bolted through him. Most days he stayed busy enough so he didn't have time to dwell on the fact his father was gone. He'd never go fishing with him again. Never sit on the boat and have a beer with him. His dad wasn't there to patiently explain how to fix some cantankerous boat engine.

He turned and looked out at the sea and let the pain just come in waves. He slowly walked into the water, knee-deep, letting it rush up to him and slowly recede. With each wave, the pain began to lessen. Tears trailed down his cheeks, but he didn't even bother to wipe them away. He didn't know how long he stood like that, but he remained until the pain had eased and he could breathe freely again.

He looked up at the sky, covered in clouds, and a sliver of light broke through and he could see a tiny hole of blue sky behind the dark gray clouds. Golden light spilled through as if there was an actual hole in heaven.

"Dad, I've missed you."

And for that one moment, he felt his father by his side, saying goodbye.

And as quickly as it had come, the hole closed up and the gray clouds covered the sky once again.

He walked out of the water and up on the beach. He picked up a shell and turned it over and over in his hand. Then he slowly raised his arm and tossed the shell into the sea. Making more of a plea than a wish.

Help me figure out my life.

CHAPTER 30

The week went by in a whirlwind for Charlotte. She flew out to L.A. and talked to Michelle Isling. She had a copy of the contract but hadn't signed yet. And she hadn't mentioned to Michelle about the conflict with the two openings. She was pretty sure if she didn't show up for the opening at Desert View Gallery that Michelle would not be very anxious to sign her.

She had to make up her mind because she couldn't be in two places at once. She stood in her studio with a fresh canvas and paints spread around her. She picked up her brush. Time to get back to her old style.

She lifted the brush and made a stroke. Then another. Then kept going. But when she looked closely at the painting, she could clearly see she was painting the waves on the sea. And pretty sure that was beach poking out at the bottom of the canvas.

She sighed and put down her brush.

What good would it be to get her name known again if she could no longer paint in her old style? It didn't feel right. Didn't feel like her anymore.

"Charlotte?" Robin's voice rang out through the bungalow.

She took off her smock and headed toward the kitchen.

"Come on. We're heading to The Nest. Girl's night."

She started to argue but, one—no one won an argument with Robin. And two—it was kind of a good idea.

They walked over to The Nest and found Sara waiting for them out on the deck. "About time. I was afraid you guys were going to miss the sunset."

Charlotte sank into a chair beside Sara and took the offered glass of wine.

Robin sat beside them and propped her feet on the lower railing. "Ah, now this is perfect."

They watched while the sky burst into

flames in long strokes of orange and yellow. "That is just stunning," Sara whispered.

They watched for a while more in silence, then Robin turned to her. "So, have you made a decision?"

"I… no… I haven't."

"You're kind of running out of time to make it, aren't you?" Sara asked.

Her phone rang, and she looked at it in annoyance. Eva. She hadn't spoken to her sister since she'd left Austin. But maybe there was something wrong with her mother again. She answered the phone, annoyed at herself for answering, but unable to just let it go to voicemail. "Hello?"

"Charlotte, so I'm headed to Palm Springs with a few of my colleagues. They go to the Palm Springs Arts Festival every year and invited me along. Imagine my surprise when I saw the brochure and *your* name was listed. I'm glad you finally listened to reason and got back to your real art."

She counted to ten, biting her lip.

"Are you moving back to California, too? I assume so. I hope this whole Belle Island phase and furniture painting is behind you now."

"You know what, Eva? I'm not going to be

at that show. I have an opening here at Paul's gallery. I wouldn't miss it for the world." And right at that very moment, she knew that she wouldn't miss it for anything. It was where she wanted to be. It was the paintings she wanted to paint. And living here on the island? Well, that was where she wanted to live.

"Why in the world would you miss an opening at Desert View Gallery for an opening on Belle Island? Don't be ridiculous. Of course, you have to go to the Palm Springs opening. My friends have already seen your name and they're expecting you."

"I have a lot of problems and things to work out... but disappointing your friends is not one of them. I'll be here on Belle Island. Not in Palm Springs."

She heard her sister click off the phone. She turned to see Robin grinning. "Guess you made your decision, then."

"Guess I did."

"Are you sure?" Sara looked over the top of her wine glass.

"I've never been so sure of a decision in my life."

"You're not just doing this to spite Eva are you?" Robin tilted her head.

"Nope. This is a decision I'm making because it's one hundred percent what I want to do. What I want for my life. I'm going to have a legal mess to clear up with the Desert View Gallery, but it is what it is." She grinned. "And I won't mind too terribly being here on the island with Ben."

Robin raised her glass. "To the new Charlotte. The one who makes decisions and knows what she wants."

"To Char," Sara chimed in.

They all three clinked glasses, and she leaned back in her chair, perfectly content with the choices she'd made and willing to deal with the fallout of those decisions.

CHAPTER 31

Ben paused buttoning up his shirt and glanced over at his phone when it rang. He didn't have much time to finish getting ready and head to the gallery. He didn't want to miss the opening. He wanted to be there to support Charlotte. And maybe they'd have a chance to talk and sort things out.

He frowned when he saw it was his mother calling. He answered the phone and put it on speaker. "Mom?"

"Oh, Ben." He could hear the panic in her voice.

"What's wrong?"

"It's Mischief. We were walking on the beach and he saw something… I'm not sure what. But he pulled on the leash and tugged it out of my hand. I've been looking for him for half an hour. I can't find him anywhere."

"Where are you?" He hurried to finish buttoning his shirt and grabbed his shoes.

"Out by Lighthouse Point."

"I'll be there in five minutes."

He tugged on his shoes and hurried out the door. She might have told him to back off and let her live her life, but when she called and said she needed his help, he would always be there for her. He glanced at the car but decided it would probably be faster to walk there and take the shortcut. He quickly jogged in the direction of the beach.

His mother waved to him when he approached. She had tears on her face that tore at his heart. "Okay, let's find this little imp of yours. Where have you looked?"

"Everywhere. I went both up and down the beach, calling for him."

"Well, we'll have to look again." He took his mother's elbow and steered her to a patch of sea oats at the edge of the beach.

"Mischief?" His mother called out. "Where are you? Mischief?"

"Here, pup." He peeked through the dense foliage.

They walked up the beach, then down the beach as the sun began to set.

"What if we don't find him before dark?" His mother's voice cracked.

His mother could not deal with another loss in her life. The silly dog just needed to be found. Who knew she'd be so completely nuts about the beast in only a few days? He pulled out his phone and looked at the time. He'd already missed the beginning of the opening, but with any luck, he'd still get there before it was all over.

They headed back to the lighthouse. As they approached, his mother broke into a run. He jogged to catch up with her. "Mom?"

"Look, don't you see?"

He looked and sure enough, Mischief was sitting on the walkway to the beach, silhouetted against the brilliant sunset.

His mother scooped up the dog, hugging him and petting him. "Oh, Mischief. There you are. You bad dog. Why did you run away? Good dog, good dog."

Good thing the dog didn't know words or he'd be confused at his mom's ramblings. "Come on, I'll walk you two home." No way he was going to let his mom walk home this late with the possibility the dog might break loose again.

"No, we'll be fine. I know you have Charlotte's opening to get to. I was going to go, too, after my walk with Mischief."

"How about we both head over then?"

He watched while his mom set Mischief down and carefully wrapped the leash around her hand, then they headed out to the gallery. He just hoped they wouldn't be too late. Because all this searching for Mischief and his mother being so full of joy at finding the dog? It had shown him how his mother was moving on from her past and beginning to care again. And it was time he did, too. He at least needed to tell Charlotte how he felt about her.

Charlotte paced back and forth at the gallery, waiting for the opening to begin. Josephine walked up to her and grabbed her hand. "Are you okay, dear?"

She smiled at Paul's wife. "I am. Just a little nervous." She laughed. "Okay, I'm really nervous."

"You'll be fine. You had great success at the local artist show, and Paul believes in you."

"And I'm grateful for all the help he's given me." She watched as Paul walked over to the front door to unlock it. "I guess it's time."

"Don't worry, dear. Everything will be fine." Josephine squeezed her hand. "I'm going to go man the refreshments. We do like a festive atmosphere for our openings."

She watched as Josephine walked to a table in the back of the gallery. A few people entered when Paul opened the door. Not many though…

She smiled and answered questions when a couple walked up to her. Slowly the gallery began to fill with people. Soon she lost track of time and began to relax.

"Charlotte?"

She whirled around at the sound of her father's voice. "Dad?"

"You look surprised."

"I *am* surprised. I didn't even think you knew about the opening." He'd never come to one of her openings. Ever.

"Eva told me about her conversation with you. How you turned down the show in Palm Springs because you were already committed to this one. That's a sign of integrity and I admire that. I thought it was high time I came to one of your shows. It looks like quite the turnout."

"I— it is. I mean. Wow, Dad, I'm glad you came." She choked back the emotions coursing through her. Her father had come to her show.

"I admit that I don't really understand your life and what you want. But I *did* listen. I know it's what you want. And if it makes you happy, then it's fine by me. I'll try to be more supportive. And… I'm really proud of you. You do really great work."

"Thanks, Dad." She had to fight to keep back tears. She'd waited so many years to hear these words from anyone in her family. Somehow, she'd come to realize she didn't need anyone else's approval, she only needed to believe in herself. But it sure felt good to hear her father say those words. That he was proud of her.

"I'm going to stick around until the opening is over. Then I need to talk to you."

She wasn't sure what that was about, but before she could ask, Sara, Noah, and Lil walked up.

"Oh, Charlotte. These are wonderful. I'm so proud of you." Lil hugged her. "I always knew you could do anything you put your mind to. Look how wonderful these paintings are."

"Thanks, Lil."

"Noah and I are going to mill around a bit. Can we bring you a glass of champagne?" Sara asked.

"No, I'm fine."

She waved at Robin and Jay when they came in the gallery. Everyone she cared about had come to celebrate her big night.

Well, everyone but Ben. She scanned the crowd, looking for him, but not a sign of him anywhere. She glanced at her watch. The opening was almost over. A lot of the crowd had cleared out. Disappointment washed over her. Didn't Ben realize how important tonight was to her? Maybe they weren't as in sync as she'd thought they were.

Then she turned and saw Ben standing in the open doorway with his mother and her dog. He hurried up to her and gave her a hug. "I'm so sorry I'm late."

Ruby walked up with her dog in her arms. "It's not his fault. Mischief got loose and I couldn't find him. Ben came to help me."

"I see you found him." She petted the dog's head, and he licked her hand.

"Yes, I'm so grateful. I seem to have fallen hopelessly in love with this little guy."

Ben kept one arm around her shoulders and leaned close. "I am sorry. I just couldn't say no to Mom," he whispered in her ear.

"You're here now." Right beside her.

"Well, I'm going to browse around and see every single painting. Mom, you want to walk around with me?"

"Do you think it's okay I have Mischief with me?"

Paul walked up to them right then. "Of course, Mischief is welcome." He petted the dog. "Good boy."

Charlotte turned to greet another couple who had questions about her work.

Later, as the gallery began to clear, Ben walked back up to her. "I'm going to walk Mom home. Could I see you later? You want to come by Lady Belle?"

"That would be wonderful."

The gallery emptied and Paul locked the door. Her father walked up to her. "You got time for that talk?"

"Josephine and I will just clear up the glasses and refreshments." Paul smiled and walked away to give them some privacy.

"What is it?"

"After you told me about your agent, I did some investigating. Delbert Hamilton spoke with me. He knows of Reginald. Reginald brokered some art for one of the Hamilton Hotels. It appears he didn't come through with what he promised. Del had been tracking him down."

"Really?" She looked at her dad in surprise.

"And we found him." He broke into a wide smile. "Let's just say he was persuaded to give back some of your funds.

He handed her a check and her eyes widened when she looked at it. "This is my money?"

"Part of it. A lot of it is gone."

"I made this money? This much?" She was in awe of the check.

"I think the rest of your funds are long gone, but at least this should help some. And Reginald is in trouble with the law over in Europe. I don't think he'll be cheating anyone else any time soon."

"Thank you." She stared at the check. "I don't know what else to say."

"Say you'll deposit the check and keep painting this art that makes you happy."

She gave her father a big hug, even though

they weren't a hugging family. He wrapped his strong arms around her and hugged her back. She couldn't remember ever getting a hug from the man.

"Now, I'm staying at Charming Inn for a few days. Going to catch a round or two of golf. Besides, your mother is busy with that charity event and she's having a ladies luncheon at the house. Better to just stay out of her way."

"I'm so glad you came."

"So, how about dinner tomorrow night?"

"That would be great, Dad."

Her father walked out of the gallery and she went over to Paul and Josephine. "Can I help with the cleanup?"

"No, dear. You were the featured artist. You don't need to help with this. Paul and I will get it all taken care of."

Paul nodded toward the door. "It was good of your father to come."

"It was. I was surprised to see him."

"He talked to me a bit. Sounds like he's very proud of you. He really seemed to enjoy your work."

She still couldn't get over the fact that her father had come to the opening. Maybe it was a new beginning with him. Even if she never got close to Eva, and even if her mother was always disappointed in her. Maybe, just maybe, she and her father could have some kind of relationship.

"Oh, and I spoke to the lawyer handling your contracts. He told me to tell you that the contract with Desert View Gallery wasn't valid since Reginald signed it and he wasn't actually representing you at the time. They'd sent the contract to Europe for him to sign, so he was long past repping you. And, long story short, you won't be having a legal hassle with them."

She hugged Paul. "Oh, thank you. I've been so worried about clearing up that legal mess."

"Well, the mess is gone." Paul smiled.

"You run along, dear. You must be exhausted." Josephine smiled at her. "It was a wonderful opening."

Paul let her out of the gallery and she stood for a few moments on the sidewalk, taking in the sweet evening air, glancing at the street lamps tossing their golden light on the walkways.

It had been quite a night.

She turned to see Ben coming around the corner and she broke into a smile. He hurried up to her and wrapped his arms around her. She leaned against him, feeling his heart beating against her cheek. She finally looked up at him. "I thought I was meeting you at the boat."

"Couldn't wait that long to see you." He grinned. He took her hand in his and they headed to the marina.

CHAPTER 32

They settled on Lady Belle with a bottle of wine to celebrate Charlotte's opening. The stars danced in the sky above them as she leaned against Ben, feeling his warmth seep into her.

"I see your father came to the opening."

"He did. He said he was proud of me. He's never said that before."

"I'm happy for you, Charlotte." He tightened his hold around her.

She grinned up at him. "I'm kind of happy for myself right now. The opening. My father… and… you. Being here with you."

He let out a deep breath and cleared his throat. "So… ah…"

She looked at him expectantly.

"Well... Jay told me that I should tell you how I feel about you."

Her heart did a double beat in her chest. "He did? And how *do* you feel?"

"I feel—I care—" He raked his hand through his hair. "I care about you, Charlotte. A lot. I know I've given off mixed signals and I've been on again off again... but the truth is? You make me happy. I'm never more content than when I'm with you. It's like... it's like you make my life make sense."

She sat there, her heart pounding, waiting for him to finish.

"So... do you know?" He stared into her eyes, searching.

"Do I know what?"

"How you feel about me?"

"I sure do." She nodded emphatically. "Because the truth is, somewhere along the line, I've fallen in love with you."

His eyes sparkled. "You are? You do? Love me, I mean."

"Yes, Ben Hallet, I love you."

He let out a long sigh. "That's really good, because I love you, too."

Then he leaned in and gave her a kiss that

said more than their words. A promise for the future, to see what it held in store for them.

Dear Reader,

I hope you enjoyed Two of a Kind. If you want to continue on in the series try Three Little Things - Book Three in the Charming Inn series. Read more about Sara, Charlotte, and Robin along with Aunt Lil and Ruby. Oh, and the knitting group at the community center finally gets a name!

And if you missed the Lighthouse Point series you can get book one in that series, Wish Upon a Shell.

Do you want to be the first to know about exclusive promotions, news, giveaways, and new releases? Click here to sign up:

VIP READER SIGNUP

Or join my reader group on Facebook. They're always helping name my characters, see my covers first, and we just generally have a good time.

As always, thanks for reading my stories. I truly appreciate all my readers.

Happy reading,

Kay

THANK YOU for reading my story. I hope you enjoyed it. Sign up for my newsletter to be updated with information on new releases, promotions, give-aways, and newsletter-only surprises. The signup is at my website, kaycorrell.com.

Reviews help other readers find new books. I always appreciate when my readers take time to leave an honest review.

I love to hear from my readers. Feel free to contact me at authorcontact@kaycorrell.com

COMFORT CROSSING ~ THE SERIES

The Shop on Main - Book One

The Memory Box - Book Two

The Christmas Cottage - A Holiday Novella (Book 2.5)

The Letter - Book Three

The Christmas Scarf - A Holiday Novella (Book 3.5)

The Magnolia Cafe - Book Four

The Unexpected Wedding - Book Five

The Wedding in the Grove (crossover short story between series - Josephine and Paul from The Letter.)

LIGHTHOUSE POINT ~ THE SERIES

Wish Upon a Shell - Book One

Wedding on the Beach - Book Two

Love at the Lighthouse - Book Three

Cottage near the Point - Book Four

Return to the Island - Book Five

Bungalow by the Bay - Book Six

CHARMING INN ~ Return to Lighthouse Point

IN 2020

One Simple Wish - Book One

Two of a Kind - Book Two

Three Little Things - Book Three

Four Short Weeks - Book Four

Five Years or So - Book Five

SWEET RIVER ~ THE SERIES

A Dream to Believe in - Book One

A Memory to Cherish - Book Two

A Song to Remember - Book Three

A Time to Forgive - Book Four

A Summer of Secrets - Book Five

A Moment in the Moonlight - Book Six

INDIGO BAY ~ Save by getting Kay's complete collection of stories previously published separately in the multi-author Indigo Bay series. The three stories are all interconnected.

Sweet Days by the Bay

Or buy them separately:

Sweet Sunrise - Book Three

Sweet Holiday Memories - A short holiday story

Sweet Starlight - Book Nine

ABOUT THE AUTHOR

Kay writes sweet, heartwarming stories that are a cross between women's fiction and contemporary romance. She is known for her charming small towns, quirky townsfolk, and enduring strong friendships between the women in her books.

Kay lives in the Midwest of the U.S. and can often be found out and about with her camera, taking a myriad of photographs which she likes to incorporate into her book covers. When not lost in her writing or photography, she can be found spending time with her ever-supportive husband, knitting, or playing with her puppies —two cavaliers and one naughty but adorable Australian shepherd. Kay and her husband also love to travel. When it comes to vacation time, she is torn between a nice trip to the beach or the mountains—but the mountains only get

considered in the summer—she swears she's
allergic to snow.

Learn more about Kay and her books at
kaycorrell.com

While you're there, sign up for her newsletter to
hear about new releases, sales, and giveaways.

WHERE TO FIND ME:
kaycorrell.com
authorcontact@kaycorrell.com

Join my Facebook Reader Group. We have lots
of fun and you'll hear about sales and new
releases first!
https://www.facebook.com/groups/KayCorrell/

facebook.com/KayCorrellAuthor

instagram.com/kaycorrell

pinterest.com/kaycorrellauthor

amazon.com/author/kaycorrell

bookbub.com/authors/kay-correll

Made in the USA
Coppell, TX
21 February 2021